LEAH & DRE

A Philly Love Story

YONA

Cole Hart
SIGNATURE NOVELS

Leah & Dre: A Philly Love Story

Copyright © 2020 by Yona

All rights reserved.

Published in the United States of America.

Published by Cole Hart Signature, LLC.

Mailing List

To stay up to date on new releases, plus get information on contests, sneak peeks, and more,

Go To The Website Below...

www.colehartsignature.com

❧ I ❧

LEAH

"*My heart so cold I think I'm done with ice, Say if I leave her she gone die. Well bitch, you done with life*" Blasted from the speakers inside of my cousin's small apartment.

I smirked, as I rapped along to DaBaby's new hit song, *Toes*, while sitting at the kitchen table. "*Say you got that sack, I got that sack. But ain't no ones in mine.*" I bent to twerk a little in the chair while swinging my twenty-eight-inch raw Indian hair.

My cousin, Shermaine, bobbed her head taking a long pull from her Newport before dealing the cards. The four of us sat around her table playing a game of spades and discussing the latest movies while occasionally singing a song or two. The fan was the only thing helping us keep cool as we drank Henny, from cups.

Everyone was looking at me, as I stood up and shook my Milano hoodie for the third time. The weed that I just smoked all to myself had me paranoid. I had seen another mouse run across the stove and had it been nighttime; I wouldn't have thought too much about it. However, the sun was beaming through the small kitchen window, and the mice and roaches were coming out like they were drinking with us.

Tugging at the top of my dark blue distressed jeans that

hugged my plumped ass like a second skin, I finally got them up so my panties wouldn't be on full display. Sitting back down, I picked up my cup and looked inside of it to make sure nothing was in it before taking a sip. The more the warm liquid ran through my body, the harder it got for me not to speak on this place. I knew Shermaine well enough to know that if I mentioned anything about her house or kids running wild while we smoked and drank, she would want to fight. So, I left it alone for now and just continued the game.

"I'm telling you, that movie was corny as hell. Tyler Perry tries to pull off that same bullshit ass plot every time, and everybody falls for it." Shermaine said with her cigarette dangling from the corner of her mouth, and her head wrapped looking like Monique on the Precious movie.

"It's not, and that just means you ain't taken the story for what it was. That man was dropping messages left and right." Shaking my head, I tossed the Little Joker on the table, winning the spade game.

"Nah, for real Leah, you know damn well that movie was below budget. That man got all that money, and they are still wearing those bum ass wigs, and everybody on the book is saying the same damn thing." Shermaine rolled her eyes.

"All I can say is watch it for yourself, Lo. I mean if you care about how people look in movies and not the story behind it you shouldn't like a lot of movies. On top of that, why do you care about what they say on Facebook? I'm sure everybody is saying something different." Grabbing the cards, I shuffled them.

Shermaine stood up and downed her cup of Patron. She walked past bringing attention to her three-year-old son, who was running around with a soggy diaper. On a good day, my cousin was just above average looking. However, it didn't take away from the many men she slept with on the regular. Her short pixie hair cut that she had covered in her head wrap complimented her round chubby face. She was what people referred to as high yellow and classified as a BBW. I guess that ran in our family because I wasn't that much smaller than her. Her body used to be curvy, but after six kids, she had let herself go.

"Girl you need to change him." Lo pointed at Joe Joe.

"Don't worry about that; he was changed. But like I was saying. Leah, you really don't think Tyler could have done better. Like he had that old man in the background eating and drinking air." She laughed.

"Yes the hell he did. Like, come on now dawg. I don't think it was his best; however, I don't think it was the worst." Jelly laughed along with her, showing her mouth full of braces.

"That's why I posted that meme today about how he basically puts black women down. He makes us seem so vulnerable, and then has us settling for the bare minimum." Shermaine went on.

I rolled my eyes as I listened to her downplay the movie. Glancing around, I noticed just how messy my cousin's house was. Her dishes were piled up to the ceiling and all over the counters. Dirty diapers lay on the floor next to the trash can.

"What you rolling your eyes for you know damn well it's true. Facebook is on point with everything." Shermaine lit up another cigarette while changing the baby on top of the deep freezer.

I watched as Shermaine switched over to the sink and grabbed the dishrag to wipe the shit that had smeared on the deep freezer before tossing it in the sink. Frowning my face up with disgust I was glad to have brought paper cups because this bitch was nastier than I thought.

"Let's just get back to the card game." Jelly stood and pulled a wedgie out.

Her body was sick, and the hoodie dress that she had on barely covered her round ass. Her face had a few bumps on it, but that didn't take away from her looks. Her cat eyes gave her an exotic look, and her simple outfit looked everything but simple. However, just like my cousin, she was nasty. Had it not been for my sister asking me to meet her over here an hour ago I wouldn't be here. Looking down at my phone, I sent Amelia another text telling her to come on.

"Why is Facebook so credible to you? I don't get how it's a bunch of people trying to pick apart that man for whatever reason. Nobody goes off their own opinion anymore?" I frowned.

Shermaine, sucked her teeth as she sat Joe Joe, on his feet.

"Facebook is credible well to me anyway, and if you paid more attention to it, you would know just how much it was." She snickered with Jelly.

Throwing my head back, I had to look at the ceiling and count roaches. I just knew that it was shade she was throwing, and that was the main reason I tried not to step foot in this bitch's apartment.

"What are you trying to say? Cause if I were you, I would have said that shit instead of having inside jokes with the next person." I stated as calmly as I could. I was no fighter, and I wouldn't act like it. However, if need be, I could get down with the best of them.

"I mean if you want to know." Shermaine started.

"Nope, mind your business don't go there." Lo stood up.

"Nah, let this bitch go there. I mean if you got some shit for me let me have it. Cause if we speaking on people, then I could say a lot about you." I reminded her while remaining in my seat.

"If that's the case, miss high all mighty. What I wanted to say is that had you been on Facebook you would see how your man posted up in the same apartments you frown ya face up at with the next bitch. Yea, he doing all that while you think you are living this amazing life that makes you better than us. What, cause your ass finally grew, and you got some little titties now? Or because you finally learned how to go and get your hair done? Or is it because these niggas feed you bullshit about how good you look to them? You came from the same place as us, and let's not forget your drunk, cracked out ass daddy had you and your hard-working mother living worse than us. Your husband even came from here, and just because he married you and moved you out the hood don't mean you got your fairytale. 'Cause he be right back over here like he never left." She spilled as she poured a can of ravioli in a pot.

In all honesty, I wanted to pull out my phone and confirm what she was saying. I even wanted to cry. However, I wouldn't dare give these bitches the satisfaction.

"I think I'm better than you? Bitch I am you up in here smiling in my face and spilling tea. That's gone do what to make you feel better? You think you got one up on me? Okay if he cheated then hey at least he wasn't as bold as your kid's' dad who had the bitch living in your nasty ass apartment. Had you eating coochie like you were the Cookie Monster. Now if you applied that same amount of energy to them kids, finding a job, and cleaning this nasty ass place, you wouldn't be so hype to spread my business." Standing up, I grabbed my bag, ready to go.

Shaking off my hoodie, I placed it over my arm and headed towards the door.

"Oh no bitch, you think you were gone, try and read me my rights the bounce? That's not how it goes, yeah Joe did what he did and so what. But bitch let's not throw dirt like Nymir ain't fucking Jelly." She yelled.

Spinning on my feet, I almost got whiplash as I headed back over to her.

"Fuck you and fuck this big ugly bitch too. Ain't no way in hell we fucking the same nigga. Look at her. Maybe she sucked his dick but him slinging dick her way imagine that. Now since you want me to know about Jelly so bad tell Jelly to help you feed them kids bitch. Give me my can of ravioli back, fuck you thought this was? You ain't gonna talk shit like I ain't nobody all the while feeding them kids the shit I brought." I started being as petty as I could.

"Fuck you and these ravioli." She snapped, grabbing the pot off the low fire. She threw the whole pot my way.

Thinking quickly, I stepped to the side, causing some of the sauce to splash on my arm. Had it been hot, my arm probably would have gotten burned. Spinning my keys, I ran up on her and sprayed her big ass in the face with my mace. Grabbing her by her hair, I began to punch her in the back of the head.

"Get this bitch off me. I can't see." Shermaine yelled while covering her face.

"Y'all bitches bet not touch me either." I growled while slinging her to the floor and kicking her in the head.

"Stop, please," Shermaine begged.

Joe Joe and the other kids who must have come out of their room began to cry and scream, so I let her go.

"Bitch you better be lucky them kids came out and got to crying. Jelly, I'm gone see you hoe, and that's on me." I pointed out as I grabbed my shit for the second time.

Slowly walking back toward the door, I backed all the way out not wanting to turn my back to them hoes. I could hear Shermaine screaming for them to get her some water as I headed to my car.

Shermaine was a big-time hater, and for her to be my cousin, she should have let me know what it was with her friend and my husband when it first happened.

At the age of twenty-six, nobody let me forget where I had come from. Hell, I hadn't forgotten either, which was why I bust my ass every day as a receptionist at the hospital. I had no plans on going back to the place that I tried hard to forget. Yes, I had ass for days and the men that chilled around the hood let me know day in and day out just how good I looked now. While all the females figured I only had Nymir because of the girl I grew into. Back in the day, I wore braces to fix my crooked teeth, and my hair was short and nappy. Now, I knew how to fix my weave as well as go to the shop and get my hair done, O had went years without a perm and now had a nice length of hair. My braces were long gone, and my teeth were straight and pearly white, and to top it off, my butter pecan skin was blemish-free. I stood at five foot, four inches while weighing one hundred and seventy pounds. My breast were a little more then a handful however I made up for it in the ass and hips department. I had always been very pretty but the flaws I used to have made me feel ugly. Yet, that girl I used to be was long gone and you couldn't tell me that I wasn't beautiful.

Starting my car, I pulled off and headed home. While driving, I dialed my sister's number.

"I'm about to pull up now." She lied easily.

"Bitch no you not, and I'm not there anyway. So whenever you hop off the dick and wash ya ass come by my place. I gotta wash the cigarette smoke and filth off of me." I replied angrily.

"Oh god, what the fuck done happened? And I hope you shook your shit before you got in your car." She laughed.

"That shit is not funny. You had me in there for over an hour and your ugly ass, yuck mouth ass cousin just had to fuck with me like she always does. I swear I should have beat that bitch with the pot she threw at me." I hissed into the phone.

Turning onto my block, I hopped out of the car and jogged up the steps.

"Hey, Leah." My neighbor waved.

"Hey." I waved back while slowly twisting the knob and entering my house. Just as she went to say something else, I closed the front door.

I wasn't trying to be rude, but I wasn't in the mood for a long conversation.

"Girl let me call you back," I whispered then hung up without getting a response.

I could hear Nymir laughing on the phone. He had to have had his phone on speaker or a face time call because I could hear the female voice as well. I made my way to the kitchen and stood on the opposite wall.

"Who the fuck is that? And what the fuck is this I hear about you fucking the girl that lives next to Shermaine?" I snapped.

Nymir hung his phone up and then looked at me. His handsome chocolate face that I loved so much was looking ugly to me at the moment.

"Who the fuck told you that?" He asked with a deep frown.

"That don't matter. Let me know what the fuck is up? Then you got a bitch on the phone in my house. I'm this close to leaving your ass." I fussed, stepping into his space mushing him.

"Look, whoever said that shit is lying to you. I swear on my grandmom's grave. I ain't fuck nobody over that way in a while." He rubbed his hands over his face.

While I wanted to believe him, my gut feeling was telling me different. My mind was also telling me to knock the shit out of him for disrespecting me.

"I'm gonna find out the real and when I do you better hope you have a place to stay," I promised I walked away from him to do my own investigation on the situation.

He'd better hope like hell I didn't find anything out because if I did this marriage as well as the family we built with our two kids was over.

2

DRE

"Get up Dre, that damn alarm clock keeps going off," Mirra yelled while standing over me in her bra and panties.

"Damn, baby come here," I smirked, pulling her on top of me.

Her round ass and flat stomach were on display. Her titties were spilling out of her bra and even though she had just gotten up, my baby looked edible.

"Come on. I have to go get my shot in a few hours. You know we can't have sex before I get it. I ain't taking no chances." She whined.

"Man, fuck that shot. You are about to be my wife, so giving me a baby shouldn't still be a problem." I spoke with my face buried in between her breasts.

Wrapping my hands around her, I unhooked her bra, letting her breasts fall out. Sticking my tongue out, I let it travel from her nipple to her neck.

"Mmm, stop." She moaned.

Mirra grabbed my head and held it away from her. My soldier was standing at attention and wanted nothing more then a release before I headed to work.

"Come on and give me my pussy. Stop playing." I groaned.

"No, Dre. You know I'm not playing as much as I would love too I can't. I don't want to risk getting pregnant. Ain't none of my fans on the gram gone want to see me all big. I can't model pregnant, it's no way in hell." Mirra replied while pulling my hands off of her.

"Is you serious right now?" I questioned with a raised eyebrow.

"Very, don't stop my money. You ain't stopping yours." She stood up.

"That ain't even got no real fucking job. You model on Instagram for followers, and you do promos okay, I'm making thousands as a bank investor. I take care of you, you only spend those checks on shopping. I handle the bills and all, you want me to give you everything you want and need. But you can't sit your hot ass down for a few months for me." I asked while rubbing my temples.

"No, I will not mess my body up for a baby. You knew what it was before you asked me to marry you. I don't give a damn what you take care of. You thought sticking dick in me was gone be free." She pointed a long nail in my face.

"Man, move. Had you not said you would give me my child once I put a ring on it, as well as all that half-naked shit on Instagram would stop your dumb ass might not even have a ring at all." I snapped.

"Fuck you, don't talk about what I do. How about let's talk about what your ass doesn't do. Your ass is barely home. All you do in that office is kiss Mr. Harold's ass for a promotion. Imagine what would happen if we actually had a child. You think I'm gone be home alone making bottles or up all night while you sleep? You have a child that should be enough." Mirra screamed at him.

Climbing out of bed, I walked out of the room, completely ignoring her while she still talked shit. I wished like hell she would have expressed those very feelings before I got down on one knee. She knew I wanted a son more than anything to complete my family.

Stepping into the shower, I let the water run down my body and wash away my thoughts. I scrubbed myself clean and stepped out. Standing in the mirror, I took myself in. Here I was a good man at the age of twenty-seven with a college degree and a good job. I could have easily been in the streets. Hell, I came from there and did my fair share of work in those same streets to get me through college. However, I took the hard way out and made something out of myself.

I had my mom's house built from the ground up while I stayed in one of my many rental properties. One day when I was married and had my entire family, I would allow my wife to build the house of her dreams. I had been with Kamirra for four years, and just like any other man I fell for her good looks. She had the perfect body and it was sculpted as if she went under the knife. Her hair was cut into a short cut; however, she kept a long weave flowing down her back.

Kamirra's dreams were to be a model from the beginning. I knew it and supported it. Even after she started posting half-naked pictures for people's flyers, I still supported her. I even took some of her pictures sometimes. However, things were starting to get old, and I didn't see her trying to progress outside of Instagram.

After handling all my morning hygiene, I walked out of the bathroom, fully dressed and ready to start my day. Heading down to the kitchen, I wasn't surprised when I saw an apple and a bottle of water on the counter. Even though we had a fridge full of food, nothing ever got cooked unless I did it or my mother came over.

Grabbing the water, I headed out of the house ready for another long day at work. Hitting the unlock button to my Range Rover I hopped in and turned on Meek's new song *Believe*. Pulling off, I drove thirty minutes to my job.

Stepping out of my car, I had to look at my reflection in the window. Pulling my brush out, I went over my waves one last time. I smiled at the man that I had become. I still had the same boyish look however, my full beard made me look more manlier. My brown eyes and plumped set of lips was something the ladies always fell for. I stood a little over six foot tall with a well-built body. I kept my hair cut show casing my deep waves. The gray Armani suit went great against my dark-colored skin. Fixing my tie, I headed into my office with one thing on my mind. And that was my promotion. I had spent countless nights inside of Harold & Co investment bank, trading money with buyers and sellers. On an average week I was working sixty hours, and it was taking a toll on my fiancé and my life. However, if I got the promotion to become a managing director, I could get another day off.

"Marcus, let me up. I need to get into DreQuan's office, and I know his ass is in there. He is always here, that's why he can never take care of his daughter." I heard my baby mom, Shay yelling.

"Damn, you just ain't cutting a nigga no slack today huh?" I mumbled.

"Oh there he goes, Dream, gone head over there with ya daddy. I got a damn flight to catch and your late." She placed her hand on her hip.

"Shay, can we talk outside please," I asked, keeping my composure.

Shay turned on her heels and stomped out of the building. My daughter and I followed quickly behind her. She stopped walking once she got to her car and looked at me. I opened her door and sat my daughter inside before closing it.

"Didn't I tell you stop coming to my fucking job yo? You in there causing a fucking scene when I told you to drop her the fuck by my moms last night and I would get her after work today." I scolded.

"The fuck you mean, your mammy ain't make her we did. So what does she need to watch her for? You can do it. I told you that I had a flight to catch at twelve, and you are about to make me late. Now get ya damn daughter so I can leave." She rolled her eyes while placing her hand on her hip.

I looked at her and took in her body. You could say I had a type because she looked real similar to Mirra. Her short frame came up to my chest, and her hair was straight with a middle part that hung over the top of her plump ass. Shay exotic facial features made her look like she was mixed with something, but she wasn't. Her skin-tight shorts did nothing to hide that fat pussy from being on display.

"Man, because I have a fucking job. It's nine in the morning. I have to work to pay that high ass child support you got me on all the while I still supply for my daughter outside of it. Now take yo ass on for you have a problem." Opening the back door I got my daughter's hand and prepared to walk back into the building.

"Yeah okay, and if you keep looking at me like you were just doing, I ain't gone be the only one with a problem. I'm sure Mirra would hate to know her man is still looking at me like he wants another taste." She smirked.

I had to chuckle while walking off, that girl was crazy. She knew I wouldn't touch her ass with a sick dick. Shay was a hoe and was proud of it. My baby mom was well known at the abortion clinic, and she didn't have a problem with sleeping with any nigga she saw coming up in the game. That's exactly why we didn't work out. While I was away at college trying to better our situation, she was at home getting smutted out.

Imagine my surprise when I came home for spring break and walked into my mom's apartment to see her in my bed getting fucked by another man, while my daughter sat in her crib looking. That right there almost got me time in jail as well as made me leave her.

"Daddy, I missed you." Dream said, breaking me from my thoughts.

"I missed you too, I'm going to have to see if Mom-Mom can

pick you up until I'm done with work. Tomorrow's Saturday and I have an early day. We can go to the mall if you want." I promised.

"Okay, when is my mom coming back? I forgot my iPad because she was rushing." She frowned.

"I think Monday, that's what she said and you have your laptop at my house, remember? Did you bring your homework?" I asked her while we headed up to my office.

"Yeah, I got it. I was gone do it while I waited for grandma to come." She smiled, showing all of her teeth that were still growing in.

Dream was the perfect mixture of Shay and me. She had her mom's deep dimples and my pouty lips. She had a nice butter pecan complexion and was short for her age. At seven, most of the kids towered over her making her hate her small size.

"I passed my sight word test today. I got one word wrong. I couldn't spell anything important for nothing. I was stuck on it, and then I forgot one letter." She sighed, kicking her feet up.

"Long as you tried and did your best I'm proud of you. Now hush up, I got to get a start on this work or I'm gone be here extremely late." I told her as I opened up my files.

I saw that I had a meeting in less than an hour with a couple about their stocks. They were easily going into debt, and I had to show them why. There was a soft knock on my door.

"Come in," I called, looking up from my computer.

"Mr. Wilson, we have a company meeting at eleven, Mr. Harold said to come and let you know." Marsha, Mr. Harold's assistant, spoke sweetly.

"Okay, you mind telling him I have an appointment at ten, I'll try and finish up as early as I can with them." I replied.

"Cool, and your daughter is beautiful, she looks just like you." She winked.

"Thank you." I forced a smile.

Marsha closed the door and Dream let out a loud laugh.

"Daddy, that lady liked you, and you almost frowned at her for being nice." She shook her head.

"I said thank you." I shrugged just as my mother walked in.

"Come on, baby. Your daddy's clients are on their way up." My mom said after she kissed my forehead.

"Good looking Ma, love y'all." I thanked my mom.

She smiled as they rushed out. I pulled up their files and got myself ready. If I could fix this couple's problems, I knew the promotion was mine. So I was going to put my all plus some into helping them.

❧ 3 ❧

LEAH

Climbing out of bed, I sucked my teeth. Here it was five in the morning, and again, my husband was not in bed. I hit the button on my phone to silence my alarm and then went to wake my kids up for school.

"Callie, baby wake up." I tapped her until she rolled over.

"Morning, Mommy." She smiled her toothless smile.

"Morning baby." I returned her smile.

Once she was out of bed, I walked down the hall to get Cion up. To my surprise, he was up and fully dressed, playing the game with his dad.

"Good morning, Cion, come on and eat," I said, pulling his attention away from the game.

"I ate cereal already." He replied.

Nodding my head, I walked out and headed back to Callie to help her get ready for school. While Cion looked like his father, Callie was all me. Her butter pecan skin was the same as mine as well as her sandy brown hair, and honey brown eyes.

"Callie baby, what you want to wear today." I asked while looking at her messed up ponytail.

"This." She grabbed the most colorful outfit she could find from her closet.

Deciding to help her hoping it would make the process much faster, I grabbed a pair of jeans and let her keep her shirt. I could hear the rain falling outside, so I grabbed her rainbow-colored rain boots. I took her to the bathroom and wiped her down before getting her dressed.

"Mommy, my birthday coming?" She asked with a bright smile.

"No, Callie, your birthday has already come. Remember your unicorn party. Next year it'll come again, and you will be five." I pinched her cheeks then sat her up on the counter.

"Okay." Callie pouted.

We both brushed our teeth then went downstairs so she could have a pop tart. It was no use in cooking since Cion had already eaten.

I checked the weather on my phone before scrolling through all my social media accounts. Though I had deactivated my Facebook awhile ago, I found myself opening my page back up. What Shermaine had said about Nymir had been on my mind, and I just had to see for myself. Scrolling through her page, I didn't find anything, so I looked through her friends to see if anyone looked familiar. Without a name, I was going on a blind search.

"Yo, Cion wants to go to the bounce house later, you want to go?" Nymir asked, scaring the shit out of me.

"Yeah, yeah that's cool," I said while closing my Facebook app.

"Fuck you doing that you ain't hear me talking to you? Why did you close your phone screen so fast? You talking to somebody or something?" He shot question after question.

"Don't question me about my phone when you don't want me questioning you about yours." I frowned at him.

"Why do you want to do this right now? Just answer my question, Is that somebody you are talking to?" He tried to grab my phone.

"If it is, that's none of your concern. Go question them

project bitches you just can't seem to leave alone." I rolled my eyes.

"Ain't nobody worried about them, I swear since we've been married I ain't cheat on you. I had conversations with females, but we were just friends, that's all." He lied.

"Yeah okay, come on so I can get y'all to school." Standing up, I walked to the door and waited for Callie, and Cion to come over with their book bags.

Nymir kissed both their foreheads. I watched him with a deep scowl on my face. Our family was fucked up, and we argue so much our kids were used to it. I remember when they used to cry now, they just got their stuff and sat quietly or went to their rooms. It hurt my heart to realize that maybe just maybe we were falling apart.

My family was starting to remind me of the very family I didn't connect myself to. My mom was a beautiful lady, but her heart was cold. She didn't give one fuck about her kids which made me into the overprotective mother that I was. She didn't care about anything but her man, that was until he left her and went back to his wife. Once he left her, she basically left us to fend for yourself.

My daddy is who I liked to call *Casper the friendly ghost as a kid.* It wasn't until I got older and found out that the man I knew as my father wasn't my biological dad. My mother did a good job of making everybody believe her crack head husband was my father. My mom wouldn't even tell me who I really belonged to. She would say "if he wanted you to know him, you would." Hell at this point it didn't make a difference because I never had a father anyway. Eventually, I gave up and just accepted the fact I would never know, and I was cool with that.

My sister was the complete opposite of me. What we went through, made me want to have the perfect family and be the best mom and wife I could be, while also giving my kids a loving two-parent home. She, on the other hand, opted to never want kids in fear of putting them through the same thing we went through. Amelia was a hustler by nature and made money any way she could. It was as if she made money in her sleep, that girl was into any and everything. She was so carefree and often I wanted to get a taste of that.

"Cion, gone head and get in the car and buckle your seatbelt," I told my son while helping Callie.

"Dad, I thought you said you were gone. Let me go with you so I can sit in the front." Cion frowned.

"I got plans big man, next time," Nymir said before walking to his own car.

I remember wanting a man to wine and dine me. I remember wanting someone to open my doors and pull out my chairs. However I felt like those types of men didn't exist. Nymir hadn't even waited for me to get into my car before he was pulling off.

Starting my car, I frowned when the engine light came on. I knew for a fact Nymir had told me he had taken it to the shop to get my new radiator installed.

Pulling off, I headed towards my kids' school. Hearing the familiar singing sound, I looked down at my dashboard to see my car was still overheating.

"Fuckkkk." I let out in frustration.

"Mom, your car is smoking again," Cion stated, pointing out the small cloud of smoke.

Pulling over on the side of the road, I cut my car off. I got out of the car after popping the trunk and headed to the back of the car. Just like I thought the brand new radiator I had purchased a week ago was still in the trunk.

"This is bullshit." I barked while slamming the trunk closed.

Getting back inside the car I called on my sister for help. She happily agreed; however, I knew it was a long lecture to come with her picking me up. Amelia swore up and down she didn't judge people however, she always felt the need to explain to them how she would handle things. After waiting ten minutes, she pulled up. Grabbing the kids and our things, I climbed into her car.

"I thought Marvin ordered that piece for you that you needed?" She said, looking over at my car.

"He did," I replied.

"So why the fuck is your car not fixed? Aleah, you have a damn job and kids who are in school. There's no reason for you to not have gotten that done as soon as the part came. I even gave you Jerome's information, who said he would put the piece in for free. Don't tell me I slept with him for nothing." She fussed.

"Girl, that's too much and my babies in here." I looked back at them.

"They ain't worried about shit I'm saying they got them damn tablets with the earphones up. Now tell me why the fuck your car ain't running." She rolled her eyes.

"Just drive, and because Nymir said he was gone take it while I was at work. Jerome gave me a day and time too. And it wouldn't interfere with my schedule. I guess Nymir's ass never took the fucking car, but he told me he did. He could have just said that he wasn't gone take it or that he couldn't, and I would have dropped it off and caught a damn Uber to work." I sighed.

"You keep depending on that man. I ain't gone tell you nothing cause you don't care what I have to say, but I'm gone say it anyway. He ain't doing shit that he couldn't take it. I fuck with multiple drug dealers some that are on a higher level than him, and they make time for what they want to make time for. On top of that, I don't understand why I even had to reach out to Jerome when Nymir's brother works in a damn shop." She stressed.

"Listen, can we discuss some other shit. I'm already running late on getting the kids to school, and I have to be at the damn doctor's for my TB shot in an hour." I groaned.

"That's your problem now, instead of handling your shit when it first happens you want to wait. I'm not telling you anything wrong, Leah, I love you more than life itself. You were my first real-life baby doll, and you have my babies. I'll always be here for you anytime you need me. However, I also need you to know that I'm gone be the one to tell you when I feel like you're slipping. That's your husband, you love him, and you're willing to do whatever to keep your happy family, including losing yourself as well as your happiness. Is he willing to do the same thing, though? You deserve the world baby nothing less, and you shouldn't settle for anything less." She scolded.

"I know you love me and I love you too Mi, I just can't walk away cause shit got rocky. Can you see if Jerome can pick up my car, I got paid earlier today? And I can pay him for the pickup." I asked, poking out my bottom lip.

"Don't worry about that, I have my spare key. It'll get done today. Just be prepared to catch Ubers or wait for me." She said as she pulled up to Cion's school.

"Come on boy, hurry up before ya late," I said while jumping out of the car.

We ran up to his building, and I let his hand go so that he could go inside the school. Once he was inside, I went back to the car and stayed silent the entire ride to Callie's daycare.

"You don't have to wait for me, the doctor's office right up the street. I can walk from here," I told Amelia.

"Okay, call if you need me. Love y'all." She yelled through the window.

"Love you back." I waved.

Once I got Callie checked in at school. I walked the few blocks to the clinic to get the shot I needed. I sat quietly in the waiting room scrolling through Facebook. For some reason, I was asking God to give me a sign because this was going to be the last time he cheated on me, and I did not either leave or get even. I was so tired of being the only one hurt. I chewed hard on my bottom lip, almost drawing blood as I looked through Shermaine's friends and tried to find something for the second time today. My heart rate increased when I clicked on a page only to find nothing.

"Aleah Gavins." A nurse called from the back.

Getting up, I followed her to a small room.

"Hello, I'll be doing your TB shot, I'll give you papers stating that you had it done.

You have to come back in two days just to get a reading to see if it's negative or positive." She smiled.

"Okay," I said while taking a seat.

It took all of three minutes before I was walking out of the clinic. I waited on the side of the street for my Uber to pull up. Even though it was my day off, I headed to my job at Building Leaders preschool to drop my paperwork off. Once done with that, I headed home to clean and start dinner. With every break I found myself on social media looking for a sign of my husband cheating however, I found none. Eventually, I deleted the Facebook app again. If it was meant for me to find something I would have. However, right now must have not been the time.

4

DRE

"Dream catch the ball, keep your eyes open," I called out to Dream.

We were in the park playing catch, and she kept closing her eyes each time the ball got close to her. I had to laugh when the ball knocked her sunglasses off the top of her head.

"Dad, I'm a girl. You are throwing the ball at me like I'm a boy. I don't play football. I like to paint my nails and look cute." She frowned.

"My bad, one day when you have a little brother you still gone have to play catch just with both of us and not all the time. Cause we can't paint no nails." I told her.

"Yeah, well if you would have brought your girlfriend she and I could have done nails. But she had to work? Where does she work any way that she stays in the house to do it?" Dream asked.

"She's a model," I replied, catching the ball.

"Well, where's the camera person? Or does she do pictures for Instagram like mommy? Because she has a bunch of them up there, I see her on my mom's page all the time. I love Instagram, daddy. I know you do baby. Then you know I'm not really into the park dad, I would much rather be somewhere shopping or something. You know money is EVERYTHING." Dream told me with a bored expression.

"Let's just enjoy our time together. Look here comes the ice cream truck. We can grab some and sit down and go over your spelling words. Or just talk about anything. Look I know ya pops a little boring to you because we can't go get our hair done together or go to the nail salon.

"Plus we ain't always going to the mall, you like to spend up all my money," he said jokingly. Maybe if you got a job and had some money of your own we could, but right now we need to bond babe. Bonding time is about spending time with people wherever you are just having fun creating memories that you will never forget. Don't ever just think bonding is about spending money. That won't get you far when you grow up in this crazy world. Some of my best friends don't have as much money as I do, but that doesn't make us not friends. Your mom has you thinking everything is about money, and having that mindset is great, but if you think money is everything and you base everything off that logic when the money's gone what will you have then?" I questioned her.

"Nothing and I ain't old enough to have a job. You said if I kept my grades up, I could have anything I want. I have all A's, and I have never been suspended or gotten into a fight. That's even more of a reason. Plus, why would I have a job when you make a lot of money dad. My mommy says you pay her bills and she doesn't have to work. So if I find a man that loves me and we have a baby, then I don't have to work." She sassed.

I had to bite my tongue because I almost cursed at her. I knew that this behavior was because of me. My mom told me time and time again that if I spoiled her, she would have this attitude as if the world was owed to her. But this extra shit came straight from her mom. One thing I wasn't gone do was have my daughter acting anything like her.

"Let me tell you one thing, and I hate that we have to discuss this at your age, but shit since you want to think your moms is right then so be it. I help your mom on the strength of you, that's all. And every man ain't like me. Don't you ever in yo life let me hear you spit some shit like that again. You are a Franklin, and we get the biggest bags we can get. I'm working so that you can go to college and make something of yourself, not for you to become a baby mama living off the next muthafucka you got that?" I scolded her.

"Yes." She nodded quickly.

"Good, now the next time we have a conversation like this you better be telling me you gone be a doctor or some shit, own some properties. I want you to be somebody's wife, I want to walk you down an aisle baby girl first, and then you start your family. Hell even if you start your family first make sure you have ya shit so that if anything falls you good, you can take care of yourself. However, you make your man be a provider too not somebody who gone leech off you." I explained.

"Come on, dad, I'm ready to go. I'm only seven. Let's talk about this concert I want to go to for my birthday. JoJo Siwa is coming, and I have to see her." She switched topics while standing up.

Smiling, I nodded at her. I was mentally preparing for the conversation I wanted to have with Shay. The more I thought about it, the angrier I got. We walked to the car hand in hand while completely silent. I helped her into the front seat and buckled her seatbelt and then climbed in.

"I put my foot on the gas, takeoff. I cannot let these boys pass me. Make a move and the scene gone get nasty. He get jammed since he wanna be flashy" Dream bobbed her head to the song *flexin' N' flashin'* while I drove us home.

After ten minutes of driving, I finally pulled into my driveway. We headed inside the house and went our separate ways. Going towards the kitchen, I looked in the sink and frowned at the dishes inside of it. I stopped thinking about coming home to a home-cooked meal a long time ago. Taking the back steps that were inside the kitchen, I went straight into my room. I found Kamirra standing in the mirror on the phone, laughing.

"What are you doing today?" I asked, causing her to jump.

"Fuck you scared the shit out of me." She held her chest.

"My bad, you ain't ordered nothing to eat?" I questioned looking at her through the mirror.

"No, I had noodles. Usually, y'all eat before y'all come in. How was your day." She questioned.

"It was cool," I said, turning the tv on.

Kamirra finished her conversation while I watched tv here, and there I looked over at her because of her frequent sniffing. Every time she did that it was a constant reminder of the times she used to sniff that powder. I forgave her after she went to rehab and got help. Being as though she only tried it a few times, it wasn't that hard for her to get off it.

I looked back over at her, thinking she would come talk to me. She was so busy doing her makeup that she didn't pay me any attention, nor did she bother to ask about Dream.

"Yo, you good? Fuck you keep sniffing for like you a damn coke head?" I asked when I couldn't take it anymore.

"Don't disrespect me like that. My nose is running. I think it's my allergies." She sniffed again.

"Blow that muthafucka then damn." I frowned, turning my attention back to the tv.

Kamirra stood up from her vanity and headed out of the room. It was then I was able to see that she was dressed for a night out. I had to double-take at the shorts she had on. Her ass cheeks were spilling from the bottom, and the silver heels she had on had her legs looking real good. As much as I wanted to complain about her outfit, admittedly she looked good, and my dick was on brick. She had on a crop top shirt that showed off her flat stomach. Getting up, I followed behind her.

"Where you headed in the small ass shorts?" I licked my lips.

"I have to promote this party tonight. I'm getting five hundred to show my face and party a little, so it's a win-win situation for me." She smirked.

"Well, let me get some before you head out," I said instead of saying what I really wanted to say.

Complaining about her not telling me wasn't going to do anything but cause an argument. So I decided against it mainly because I was trying to get my dick wet for the first time in three weeks.

"Nope." She replied, popping the p.

"No? Man, I ain't have no pussy in three weeks. I ain't trying to beat my dick again. Let me get some before you go." I begged.

"No, Ashanti, is on her way to pick me up and if I am late, that's money out my pay. I need to make a good impression if I want to keep this manager. This is our second meeting, and she's hosting this party. That girl is making almost eight racks to host a party and perform." She beamed.

I chuckled as I shook my head. "Yeah okay."

"Aye, Dream," I called out while walking through the house.

"Yeah, dad?" She came out of her room.

"Come on, let's go over to Gram's house. She always cooks." I replied, thinking of the money I had on the streets that I needed to check in on.

My legal job was a bank investor, while my side hustle was to give some of my hard earnings to local rappers who were trying to come up in the hood. I even invested in a few singers too. I did have two little cousins in the drug game, and I would help them too; however, I didn't do anything illegal. I refused to risk my career for fast money.

Once we left the house, it took all of twenty minutes before we were walking into the front door of my mother's two-story home.

"Cousinnn." My little cousin Don said while dapping me up.

"Just who I wanted to see, walk me outside right quick.

Dream go say hi to grams." I said while bumping fists with Tony, my other cousin.

I followed him out the door and stopped on the porch pulling up my sagging pants I leaned against the rail.

"Cuz, the game has been treating me real good. You one hard nigga to catch up with. I tripled your money twice, and every time I call you, you at work. I was ready to invest in some shit just to come in that bitch and see you." He told me as he blew smoke out his mouth from his black and mild.

"Man, it ain't that hard you could have dropped by my house. And why you smoke that shit man, you might as well smoke a port." I frowned in disgust.

"Fuck all that, I been past your house yesterday you wasn't there. Mirra said you took Dream to the mall. What's up with her? I be seeing her in the clubs with these coke head bad bitches. Wifey ain't on that shit, is she? Cause she be looking fucked up in these spots." Don spilled.

"She be with who? Man, her ass told me she be with party promoters some shit she be having to do for that dumb ass Instagram modeling shit she be doing. If she gets high that's something I just can't deal with. Especially with me having a child that is around her and in the crib." I sighed.

Here it was now instead of having to just talk to Shay I was going to talk with Mirra too. I was just hoping it was the company she kept doing that shit and not her.

"I can't tell you if she is or isn't. I know when the bitches grab the zip of that white girl, and they are in the club promoting and doing all kinds of wild shit. They don't be all high and stupid though, it's like they fictional coke heads." He expresses like that made it any better.

"I'm gonna see what's up with her, even if she ain't gone tell me I'm gone have to catch her in the act. Give me my money so I can go see what's up with my moms." I held my hand out.

"It's in the house I told you it's a lot of that shit why would I hand it to you out here. My nigga ya street smarts is leaving you." He laughed as he walked into the house.

I was hot on his heels. Walking through the house, the aroma of fried chicken hit me, causing my stomach to growl. So I headed straight for the kitchen to get some.

"Mom, what's up," I said, pulling my mother into a hug.

"Hey baby, how's your day and why my glam child ain't ate since lunch? That bitch still starving you over there?" My mom fussed.

"She was on her way to work," I replied.

"Showing your ass on Instagram ain't no damn job, not a real one anyway. You're a bank investor, and your fiancé just so happens to be a Instagram model slash club promoter. Lord, make it make sense for me." My mom called out to God.

"That's something you shouldn't be worried about mom. No matter what she is, I love her, and it may not be all good but she ain't stepping out on me." I was big on loyalty, and that girl was loyal regardless of what I did.

"Whatever Dre, just be careful with the hoe. When I go to church I'm gone keep praying that when the clothes leave some more on the pictures and my glams see it that she doesn't think it's okay." My mom called out.

"Aunty her ass be on full display don't it." Don came in laughing.

I snatched my money from his hand at the same time my mom snatched the blunt from behind his ear.

"Don't be embarrassing my son." She smirked.

She was the only person I knew besides her siblings that attend church and would be high as hell right afterwards. She would be doing the Holy Ghost and rolling a backwood fifteen minutes apart.

"I love you no matter what son, and you know what's best for you. I'll support you in any decision you make. Just always make sure you follow your heart and always have my baby in consideration too." She kissed my cheek.

"I am following my heart mom," I told her.

Shit at this point I didn't know if I believed myself anymore. However, I couldn't just leave her. She was loyal to me and didn't complain when my workdays got longer. That's why I prayed she wasn't getting high. I wasn't all the way sure I would leave if anything I would get her some help. She held me down, and I owed her for that.

5

LEAH

Tears came to my eyes, but I refused to allow them to fall. Here I was two in the morning sitting in a children's hospital with Callie and Cion by myself. Callie's asthma had flared up so bad that I had to bring her in for oxygen and steroids. Nymir was nowhere to be found, and I gave up calling his phone two hours ago.

I was starting to feel what Amelia was telling me. There was no way he put his family first because he would have responded when I sent him the text message explaining to him about her asthma.

He was so selfish, and nothing he seemed to do at this point surprised me. However, it hurt like hell.

A knock on the door broke me from my thoughts, and I quickly wiped my face when my mother walked in.

"Hey baby, how is she? Your sister is in the waiting area, and we both couldn't come back. I'm going to walk Cion out to her. She's going to take him back to her house so he can

31

get in a bed and I'll stay here with you until they say if she's going to go home or get admitted." My mom rubbed my head.

"OKAY, THANK YOU. TELL MI, I LOVE HER." I EXPRESSED.

"EVERYTHING'S GOING TO BE OKAY. GOD DOESN'T MAKE ANY mistakes, and he's not giving you more then you can handle this is just a battle Callie has to fight. She's strong Leah, she always has been." My mom said right before she walked out to leave me in my thoughts again.

THE RESPIRATORY NURSE CAME IN AND GAVE CALLIE AN asthma treatment. And checked her vitals while I sat quietly. Just as she finished up, her doctor walked in. They talked for a few seconds before the doctor turned to me.

"SO WE ARE GOING TO TAKE HER OFF THE OXYGEN AND SEE how she does, with just the steroids and treatment. If she can go a couple hours without needing the oxygen and can stretch out to at least four hours and be fine without a treatment, y'all can go home in the morning. I just need to monitor her for a while. If she does need the oxygen again be prepared to stay. We are going to play this by ear. I'll also need her to drink something." He said before leaving.

"WHAT DID THEY SAY?" MY MOM ASKED WHEN SHE CAME IN.

I RAN DOWN WHAT I WAS TOLD AND THEN LAID MY HEAD ON the side of Callie's bed. I rechecked my phone to see if Nymir had even read my text, but he didn't. Sitting the phone down, I sighed loudly.

"Now I try not to say nothing. I swear I try not to. I don't want to be a part of the crowd who tells you to leave your marriage, however, this is beyond that. Y'all have been married for some time now, and I know it's a lot of what he says going on in y'all marriage with him cheating. He gets by with all this stuff because you'd rather sweep it under the rug, then address it. Now I want your marriage to work, hell I've known that damn boy all his life, and he used to be so good to you. Especially once Cion came. Now at this point, we all know you ain't going nowhere including him. But baby make him think you are at least. This shit got me ready to call Nyiema and have her beat his ass. You know she ain't raised that boy like that, and you would think because his trifling ass came from a two-parent living family he would be better. I'm starting to see he ain't shit." My mom fumed.

"I know mom, and I know Ms. Nyiema, would not be pleased with him. This is one of the reasons they cut him off and don't deal with him. I can't just get y'all involved in this because the moment I forgive him y'all still be mad. This right here has changed my outlook I swear because this is his daughter this ain't about me or us. I beg him to tell me that this isn't what he wants anymore, but then he starts that crying shit saying he gone change. And if I can fix my marriage, I'll try. I'm twenty-seven with two kids that's a lot already I don't want to have a divorce on my belt as well. I'm going through all this right now, and he's nowhere to be found. This ain't right. I do good by him, I've never cheated nor stepped out on my marriage. I work, go home, and still cook and clean. And this is the thanks I get this ain't fair mom, I be feeling like giving up on all this. I can't take this no more, the kids, the hospital visits. I'm losing my mind." I cried.

"Baby, God knows what he's doing. Don't you dare give up on yourself. You keep on pushing, I raised a strong, beautiful lady. It's all gone pay off. If anybody loses you let that be him. We don't drop our heads baby even in our lowest moments we hold them high." My mom reminded me of what she would tell my sister and I when we were younger.

"I hear you." I sniffled.

Time had seemed to be moving so slow and what seemed like forever was only eight hours, and we were able to go home. I carried Callie to my car and drove straight home, not even bothering to pick Cion up.

We made it home in no time and I put Callie in her bed and then got in mines. I didn't even bother to shower I was so tired that I would have to do it later. I made sure to set my alarm to wake me so Callie could get her medicine on time. I closed my eyes and drifted into a deep sleep.

"Where the fuck you been?" Nymir yelled, waking me from my sleep.

"Boy if you don't get the fuck out my face before I knock you in yours. Don't fucking question me like you ain't get my calls or text." I sat up in bed.

. . .

"FUCK ALL THAT WHERE YOU BEEN? YOU GONE MAKE ME knock you and whoever the fuck you was with, out." He paced the floor.

"YOU BETTER GO AHEAD WITH THAT SHIT, YOU KNOW YOU ain't bout to do nothing. I was where I was at and had you picked up your fucking phone, a matter of fact if you would have brought your dumb ass home you would have known. Now do me a favor and go back to wherever the hell you came from." I stated calmly before laying back down.

"UNCLE MIR, ARE YOU GOING TO OUR BEDS TOMORROW?" Marisa and Malissa came running into our room.

I LOOKED IN BETWEEN NYMIR AND HIS TWIN NIECES. THEIR hair was into big puffballs, and they were smiling ear to ear. Their dark skin was so beautiful to me as well as their little attitudes.

"YEAH, I HAVE TO TALK TO AUNTIE LEAH, ABOUT HOW WE will set the room up and which room you'll get." He replied.

"WHAT'S GOING ON WITH THAT?" I QUESTIONED SITTING UP.

"LOOK, THEIR MOM IS IN THE HOSPITAL RIGHT NOW ABOUT TO have her baby, and Bill's wife ain't giving her none of that insurance money she got from his death. On top of that, she is getting put out of her apartment cause she has been out of work due to the problems she's been having. You know Bill was my boy, and I told him when he took his last breath I got his kids. We got extra space, so why wouldn't I give them a place to lay there head." He stressed.

"I UNDERSTAND ALL THAT, BUT YOU DON'T THINK YOU SHOULD have run that by me first? That's two extra kids we have here that means when I cook, I have to cook extra. That's extra homework and drop-offs. The proper thing to do was discuss that with me." I told him.

"DISCUSS IT WITH YOU, WHO THE FUCK DO YOU THINK YOU are? This my house, and when you leave you don't tell me shit." He snapped.

"I'M YOUR FUCKING WIFE, THAT'S WHO I KNOW I AM. I WAS AT the fucking hospital with your daughter and since this your house you make sure all the fucking bills get paid. You take care of these fucking kids, cook, clean, and when some shit gets broke, you call for it to get fixed." I yelled back, angrily.

"LOWER YOUR TONE WHEN YOU TALK TO ME. I'M THE MAN IN here, and you're going to treat me like it. Just because you paid the water bill don't mean you pay bills. I take care of the rent and all the other shit. You spend your check on what you want. As long as I have breath in my body, those girls are my responsibility. 'cause if roles were reversed, my man would have done that for me. And it's not, I told you they were getting put out. Their mom will be here to do it for them once she's out of the hospital.

She gets stamps and all that so she can provide their food." He stepped into my face.

"FUCK YOU, YOU AIN'T EVEN ASK IF YOUR CHILD WAS OKAY. You ought to pay for this shit. You the man right, so take care of your family and not just financially. I don't have any say so in this bitch, and that's fucked up. This is exactly why I should have kept my little apartment and not moved in this house with you. You yell about some shit you're supposed to do, and I don't give a damn about what your man would have done. I'm sure he would have run that shit by his WIFE first. You stand there like my fucking say so doesn't matter. Like I'm under you and not your equal." I said on the verge of tears.

"CLEARLY SHE IS OKAY, SHE IS HOME. HER ASTHMA ACTS UP ALL the time; it's not that deep. I should have been there, but I had other shit I had to take care of. You want to keep this roof over your head, right? Then here you go with that crying shit. Toughen up." Nymir grabbed his phone and walked out, leaving me in the house with the kids.

SITTING DOWN ON THE BED, I PULLED MY KNEES TO MY CHEST. Every day I felt like I should have never started a family with this man. I should have never accepted his proposal, and I damn sure shouldn't have walked down that aisle with him.

MY LIFE WAS ALL FUCKED UP, AND I DIDN'T EVEN KNOW where to start to fix it. I loved my kids; however, I felt like I rushed into a relationship just looking for love, the love I watched so many people have that I never felt. So when Nymir came into my life and showed me something new, I was dumb enough to give him my virginity, and my heart.

JUST LIKE MOST COUPLES, THE BEGINNING WAS AMAZING. HE was all about me, and once I allowed him to have his way with me, everything changed. The bitches came and so did the fights. However, I was thinking since I was the one in his house, driving his cars and on his arm, I was better than them girls when really I may have been worse off than them. He was committed to me, married to me, he owed me loyalty and all that came with a marriage. He didn't owe them girls anything, and they owed me nothing. Once I had our first child me fighting any girl that he messed with became something of the past and I didn't even bother to address the females. Him cheating became par for the course, and it didn't even hurt anymore.

I WAS MORE HURT BECAUSE I DIDN'T FEEL LOVED. I DIDN'T feel that same love I was giving. I didn't feel appreciated and most importantly, I didn't feel wanted. And to this very day, I still felt the same except it was worse. I couldn't talk to anybody because they would just say leave; it wasn't that easy. My whole life was here.

SOME DAYS I WANTED TO GIVE UP ON EVERYTHING, I STILL held my thoughts, and I could feel myself not wanting to get out of bed some days or not eating. My kids were the only thing that kept my head above water. I knew I had to pull myself together because they deserve the world, and I was going to give it to them the best way I could.

❧ 6 ❧

DRE

Pulling up to my baby mother's house, I was heated. This bitch sent me court papers to raise my child support, and I didn't understand why. I was already paying a little under a thousand dollars a month. On top of that, I got her every weekend and still brought all her clothes. When I presented that to a judge, they told me the clothes were considered gifts. However, me as a man and being able to provide for her, I never stopped. I could have just said fuck it and didn't give her shit, but child support but that wasn't in me.

Stepping out of the car with the papers in hand, I knocked until Shay swung the door open. Admittedly she looked good as hell with none of the makeup caked on and her loose-fitted house clothes. This was the Shay I fell for minus the frown she had on her face.

"Oh, you finally know where your daughter lives?" Shay said angrily.

"Yeah, I do. I just brought her home two days ago, and I talk to her on the phone every night. I only came here because I wanted to know why you requested more money from me?" I asked, rubbing a hand over my waves.

"Cause I need more, the bills are getting higher, Dream is

39

growing, summer is approaching, and she needs summer stuff, as well as summer trips." She said while placing a hand on her hip.

"Man, I could have taken her shopping, and this house is paid off thanks to my money. Every time you take her on a trip, I give her spending money, you can pay for her entry. But please tell me how are your bills getting higher? If you can't afford cable and whatever else downgrade shit get you some Wi-Fi and Netflix. Or is that still gone be too much? I questioned.

"Why can't you just give me the money to take her shopping myself?" She shot back ignoring everything else.

"Because most of that shit got spent on you just like always. A few months ago you requested more money for a tutor, Dream is a straight-A student, and she still doesn't have a tutor, so where is that money going? And you keep running to the fucking courts for everything. You are about to make me forget every-thing my mother told me and smack the shit out of you." I threatened.

"You ain't gone do shit, and if you keep playing with me, I'll make sure you can't have no visitations at your house as long as your fiancé is there now play with it." She smirked at Mirra, making me remember she was standing there.

"Bitch, you ain't gone do shit. She's just mad 'cause you gave me the ring the bitch wanted for a long time. She thought giving you a baby was gone have her walking around in my shoes. The ones Ms Snatch ya man Shay had and couldn't fill. Baby, I'm it. Give it up now if you are going to take him to court do that but don't try and take Dream away from him. You know she loves her dad as much as he loves her." Mirra smiled, flashing her ring every chance she got.

"Hoe, go head on with that whack ass speech before I put this pussy on him and give him the sons he's been dying for. Ya coke head ass ain't nothing I want to be." Shay laughed.

I looked at Mirra and frowned. I needed to see what was up with her and why everybody kept saying she was a coke head or implying that she was.

"Bitches love to assume, I ain't shit, but your baby daddy's soon to be wife and your daughter's stepmom. You couldn't fuck him if you were the last bitch on earth and God put that corny shit on a platter and served it to him. I'm it, and you'll never be. Call me what you want but don't forget to add the Mrs. bitch to it." Mirra stepped forward to get in Shay's face.

"Swear to God you not a coke head?" Shay sighed.

"Swear to God." Mirra spat.

Shay laughed before turning her attention to me.

"Agree to the adjustments, or I'll take you to custody court. I promise with the shit I have they will not allow my child to be around your bitch and that's on everything. So tell the little bitch be honest with you before you lose the very thing you love the most all the while still giving me more money like I asked for." Shay stated.

"Do what the fuck you got to do." Mirra challenged before I could open my mouth.

"Okay, that bitch just fucked up your life. See you in court, baby daddy. Your lawyer should be calling you bright and early Monday or Tuesday morning." Shay slammed her door in our face.

Sighing I walked to my car with Mirra stomping behind me yelling idle threats. I swear that girl didn't know how to keep her mouth shut. I knew all I had to do was offer Shay a few extra dollars and have her throw this shit out. Now Mirra has just fucked that up.

"What the fuck is she talking 'bout? You on that shit?" I asked while pulling off.

"No, you see me every day, have you seen me high? Come on you know I am around people who do it but just cause they do don't mean I am." She denied.

Something was telling me not to believe her. Going against my better judgement, I believed her words and just hoped she wasn't lying to me.

"Cool, I'm gone take your word, if I find out anything

different we done. Fuck that ring and all. You can make me lose my daughter behind this shit and if I did I swear to God you are dead to me and ain't no coming back after that." I told her honestly.

"I wouldn't intentionally cause no harm to you or take you out of your daughter's life. I love watching y'all bond. It's a bond I never experienced, so I would not want to ruin hers." Mirra replied, kissing the side of my face.

"I hear you," I said.

Mirra frowned and then smiled. She reached over and toyed with the zipper of my pants. Reaching her hand in she released my dick and placed her lips on it. I closed my eyes for a second until horns started honking behind us, signaling for me to go. At the moment I was thanking God for my tint because no one could see her sucking my soul threw my nuts.

"Damn, slow down." I groaned.

Mirra was doing the two hand twist while making the slurping sound. She must have been trying to take my mind off of what just happened, and she was doing a damn good job.

"Fuck." I hissed trying to keep my eyes open.

"You like that shit daddy." She asked, slapping my dick on her lips.

I watched for a second as pre-cum oozed out of my shaft and stuck to her lips. Grabbing her head, I pushed it back down and watched her bob up and down. Looking back up, I pulled onto the highway and drove a little under the speed limit. I didn't want to make her stop; however, I wasn't trying to crash either.

She propped her leg up on the dashboard and placed my hand inside of her tights. Reaching down into her panties, I found her bud and played with it making her body shake like she was convulsing. The position we were in was weird, and I was glad for my height at the moment since I was able to reach over her while she stayed latched on to my dick. She sucked me dry and then got up and wiped her mouth.

"That dick tasted so good." She smirked.

Pulling off the highway, I caught my breath before speaking.

"You were trying to make me crash?"

"Good thing you didn't. I have a hair appointment later today, and I wanted to know if you would be up for dinner? I feel like we haven't done anything as a couple lately and I miss doing that. We can even stay in and order out while we watch a movie. I just miss you so much, and you're finally not busy with work or Dream." She smiled.

"Ok, long as I can get some tonight we can do whatever. I do have work in the morning, and since nobody got that promotion yet, I'm hoping it's still an offer on the table cause I need that. My pay would go up something crazy, and I'd be able to save some more for that house I want." I replied while pulling into the driveway.

"I hope you get it too, you've been doing so much for that company it's only right it's yours. I met this up and coming rapper girl, and she's looking for somebody to invest in her. I know you have that shit you do on the side so you should check her out." Mirra said as she looked through her phone.

"Yeah? I have to see what's up. You know if she is corny I ain't even gone bother with her." I laughed.

Mirra had this way of always trying to get me to invest in people she met. Somehow they all ended up being corny as hell but cocky. I only even entertained the thought of listening to the girl, so I didn't have to hear her talk about it until I agreed.

"Okay. I am going to set something up. We can talk about business tomorrow. Today the only thing I want to do is please and cater to you. I feel like I've been slacking and I don't want to become something you are not happy with no more. And let's talk about this wedding date. When can we set that so I can offi-cially be your wife? I'm tired of just the fiancé thing at this point." She blurted out.

"When we are on the same page. Right now, it's still some shit I don't like. For example, it's cool you do the Instagram thing, but I don't want my wife naked for the world to see what's only supposed to be for me. When we have kids, I don't want them to go on social media and pull up their mom's ass. That's another thing I want a son, and you don't want kids. So, before there's a wedding, we need to figure that out." I said.

I wanted to add on finding out about her possible drug problem. However, it seemed like I would have to figure out the answer to that on my own. The last time she dabbled with some shit I had to spend three of my checks to get her into rehab and many more of them to keep her there. She promised she would never take that route again and I believed her. If I found out that she began any type of drug besides weed, it was gone be time for us to separate. I couldn't deal with a drug addict. My father was one until his dying day. Going through what I experienced at a young age was the very reason I didn't want her to become an addict.

I remember watching my father beat my mom's ass after she hid all the money and things of value in the house so he couldn't get any drugs. I also remember him pawning everything we had gotten for Christmas so he could get high, I still loved him though. The last straw for me was when he owed his supplier money, and they came into our home and beat the shit out of everybody in the house but my sister and I. That night my mom moved us out to our grandmas and never looked back. With that said, I always said I would be the best father I could be no matter what God threw my way. Sometimes I wished for a different baby mom, however, Dream wouldn't be who she was if her mother was different. My next child would be with my wife, and whether it was Mirra or someone else, I would make my family work.

7

LEAH

After everything that was starting to take place with Nymir, I couldn't seem to think straight. Everything, including the kids, was starting to frustrate me. It had been four days since the incident, and I hadn't talked to anyone yet. I was still beating myself up for staying with this man who continued to prove he wasn't for me. I didn't want to become a statistic, one of them women who was young, divorced, with kids.

I sat in my backyard, smoking weed. I hadn't smoked in a while, and here I was high as hell. Cion came running to the door, and I put the weed out and looked at him.

"Mom, the twins keep hitting me, and I'm hungry." He fussed.

"Okay, here I come." I sighed, standing up.

I walked into the house and stood in the kitchen for a second. For the last two days, I had been running behind four kids, and I could tell the twins didn't get beatings. Now usually when they came over, their mom or uncle was with them and would be in control of them; however, it was on me, and I couldn't beat someone else's kid.

"Stop jumping on the couch," I warned from the kitchen.

Just like always, Malissa kept jumping along with Cion.

Walking into the living room, I snatched Cion up by his arm and sat him down.

"Boy, don't fucking play with me. If I say sit down, you sit your ass down. You know not to jump on the damn couch. I ought to beat yo ass." I threatened. I only beat my kids when necessary and jumping on the thousand-dollar furniture that I just finished paying off would earn him a nice ass whipping.

"But you ain't say nothing to Melissa." Cion cried.

"Cion, keep running ya lips and see if I don't pop you in them." I fussed while storming back into the kitchen.

Grabbing the stuff I needed to make them peanut butter and jelly sandwiches, with some fruit on the side, I made their lunch. While they ate, I looked in the fridge at the steak I had taken out last night. However, I was in no mood to cook dinner. Closing the fridge I decided that sandwiches or cereal would be on the menu.

"Mom, I'm going to be good." Callie smiled.

"Yes, you have been being a good girl." I smiled back.

Grabbing the bottle of wine, I poured me a cup. I was going to need the whole bottle to deal with these kids. Yet, I wasn't going to drink straight from the bottle in front of them. While sipping my wine, my mind wanders off to where Nymir was. He said he had a few errands to run for his boss down at the car shop, that was four hours ago. Every day he left around the same time and came back late at night.

"I can't wait to see my new little brother. My mommy named him Nymir, cause she says God dad Nymir has been so good to us since daddy died." Marissa randomly let out make me choke off my wine.

"She named your brother what?" I asked like I didn't hear her.

"Nymir, his name Nymir Hawkins like our last name. But like god daddy's first name." She spilled.

"So now it's daddy, me and their brother all got the same name?" Cion questioned.

Grabbing my phone, I dialed Nymir's number. If this baby knew that, then he had to know that she was naming her child after him. The feelings I felt in my stomach were all too familiar, and I knew that female intuition wasn't playing tricks on me. His phone went to voicemail, causing me to slam my phone down. The front door opened and in walked Nymir and Morgan. She held a car seat while he had his phone glued to his ear.

"Mommy, can I see the baby?" Marissa ran over to her mother.

I looked in between the two with a frown. The excitement I held beforehand about this girl's baby had left when I learned the child's name.

"Hey, Ris, sit down he's sleeping," Morgan said while sitting down in the car seat.

She walked over and gave all the kids a kiss on the forehead. When she got to me, she reached for a hug, but I side-stepped her.

"What's your son's name?" I asked.

"Nymir, I asked Ny, would it be cool if I named him that and he said yeah. I thought he would have told you." She frowned looking between the both of us.

"I just don't get how you wouldn't run that by me. Like what made you think shit like that was cool? You call me sis, and you naming your son after my husband is something you let him tell me? I talked to you every day at your doctor's appointments and all." I let out angrily.

"I get that and my bad, but I ain't see nothing wrong with it." She shrugged.

"So you ain't got shit to say Nymir like you just cool with this? Cause you seem to be cool with a lot of shit nowadays. On top of that, you can be there for her while she's at the hospital, take her in and leave me here to do all this shit like what's really good?" I snapped at him.

"Man, calm down I told you what it was. She needed help,

and I helped her, that's all." He said while placing his phone in his pocket.

"So it wasn't anybody else in your family that could help?" I asked her.

"Girl no, I don't fuck with my family like that. And I'll be out of here in no time. I'm saving up to move." She said while picking up her baby.

I watched as Nymir watched her, his eyes lingered longer than I would like and he held a smile when she walked past with the baby.

"Ny Ny, you hungry?" She cooed.

Nymir grabbed him out of her arms and walked to the couch grabbing a bottle out of the diaper bag. He pulled Callie in the chair next to him, and they looked at the baby in awe.

"Hell naw, Callie and Cion go to y'all room," I yelled, making the baby cry.

"Yo, what the fuck are you doing?" Nymir growled, trying to calm the baby.

"You have me fucked up, you sitting here catering to that damn baby like it's yours. Nymir I swear to God I will fuck this place up." I screamed.

"Man, chill the fuck out this my young bull that's all." He sighed.

Morgan frowned her face up again but didn't say anything. She snatched the diaper bag up off the floor and then grabbed the baby from Nymir. She took him and the girls with her to the spare room.

"You better tell me something now. I'm so fucking sick of you. I know you fucking lying just tell me so I don't waste no more time with you. Just let me leave, and you can have that shit. I saw how you looked at her, and that look was more than your man's girl like you say. You are lying to me, I just can't prove it." I expressed.

"Why the fuck you keep pushing me. Yeah, I fucked up a few times that you know about, but I was good to you. I don't want that girl, and the only kids I have is ours. I help her because that's in me to help. I told you my guy would have looked out for y'all. Yeah, I should have run it by you, and I realized that after I talked to my grams. I love you and our kids, that's all. Those my god kids so I ain't gone see them out on the streets." He rubbed his hands over his face, then pulled me into him.

Morgan walked back out of the room, closing the door behind her. She stepped into the living and Nymir let me go. I watched as she placed her hands on her hips then looked between us.

"Okay, so I'm tired of all this shit. Nymir is lying to you. Nymir Jr is his son, and not only is he his, but so are the twins. Yes, they call him god dad because he was afraid you would leave him. I'm not about to keep putting shit behind me. We didn't move in here because I needed help. We moved in because he said you were leaving and that he was going to tell you what was really up. Not only have we been fucking around for years, but he just recently proposed to me. He already has divorce papers drawn up and is currently getting ready to file for partial custody of the kids. Now say I'm fucking lying." Morgan spat.

My words got caught in my throat as my heart raced. I wanted him to say it was a lie, but his silence confirmed everything for me. I began to sweat, and I felt like I would pass out. I had to hold on to the back of the couch to keep myself up. In that moment I knew I deserved more than what he was giving me; however, I couldn't stop the pain from flowing through my body.

"Look, I'm sorry baby." Nymir tried to explain.

"Don't fucking touch me, you want a fucking divorce, right? I'll give it to you, but don't you dare try and get my kids to be a part of this fucked up shit you created. I hate you so fucking much. I hope you die." I yelled, slapping the shit out of him.

My anger took over me, and I swung on him landing punches anywhere I could, and he just took them. Allowing me to get all my anger out. Turning around, I grabbed Morgan by her throat and began to choke her. She clawed at my hands, but I wasn't letting her go.

"Bitch I should kill you, you listened to me cry about him. You gave advice only to be one of the bitches he was messing with. You had me playing auntie to those girls doing their hair. And when DHS tried to take them, it was me who helped you get them back, and this is my thanks bitch." I yelled, digging my nails in her neck.

"Stop you gone end up killing her and go to jail." Nymir pulled at me.

I snatched away from him and stormed to our bedroom. I grabbed my bags. I couldn't believe I loved that man unconditionally, I wished I didn't, but I couldn't help that I did. I had no more fight left in me. My head was hurting as I tried to get her voice out of my head telling me those were the kids I helped get back—the kids I took in and did for like they were my own. The kids I looked at like nieces only for them to be my step kids.

Picking my gun up from out of the safe I played with it for a second. My first thought was to go out there and shoot everything moving and as I got up to do so my phone rang.

"Come help me pack the kids, and I shit. I may be going to jail because I'm finna light this bitch up." I cried into the phone.

"Leah, I'm on my way. Don't you go getting trigger happy on me. My babies need you, I don't know what's going on but you bigger than that. Don't throw your life away for someone who isn't worth it. Baby, you level up, you hear me Aleah? You do better, and you move the fuck on. It's gone be hard, but you can do it. You're strong baby, I love that about you. You're a fighter, and you always come out on top." Amelia said into the phone.

Placing my gun down, I sat down on the floor and sobbed loudly.

"Oh God, How could he do this to me. Why me God, why would y'all hurt me like this? What did I do wrong?" I cried.

"Let it out, baby." Amelia coached from the phone.

I sat there until I heard her get out of the car. Once I hung up, I stood up and began to pack more of my stuff. I needed to get out of the house and fast. Amelia came in and helped get most of our things, and I left out without uttering a single word to them. They had hurt me in the worst way, and it wasn't no coming back from that. I was leaving him, and this life and I meant it for good. That was the push I needed to go and do me.

8

DRE

My phone rang, bringing me out of my sleep. I turned over and picked it up.

"Dre, I have an overload of files on my desk today, and I need help. Do you think you will be able to come in right now and help?" Mr. Harold spoke over the phone.

"Yes, I'll be there no later than an hour," I said while sitting up in bed.

"Thank you, I'll be sure to add extra on your check for the week." He said before hanging up.

Climbing out of bed I quickly headed into the bathroom and handled my morning hygiene. Done for the week was my regular attire. I stepped into my closet and grabbed my black suit with the red tie. I took it out of the cleaner's bag and stepped into it.

Being in a suit and tie made me feel different. I didn't feel like the little boy from south Philly trying hard to make it, and get money by any means. Instead, I felt like a man that belonged, a man who took what life gave him and earned my shit the right way. I could have easily become a drug dealer and stuck with it. However, the legal money felt so much better because I didn't have to look over my shoulder to watch for the cops or somebody trying to kill me for my spot.

"Baby, get up." I tapped Mirra on her ass.

She was butt ass naked tangled up in the covers. Her make up was all over the pillowcase and she knew I hated that shit. She must have had a long night because she was drooling like hell and wasn't budging.

"Kamirra, wake up. I ain't pay all that got damn money for them modeling classes for you to miss them." I shook her instead of tapping her.

"I'm up damn." She said while turning over.

"I'm out. I have to go into work today. Call me and tell me how everything went." I told her before heading out of the house.

I got into my car and turned on the Meek Mill album *Championships* since I was feeling good and needed some motivating music to keep me up.

" *Big bag, got 'em big mad A nigga gettin' to some money and his bitch bad...Jumpin' out the Rolls truck with the temp tag... I'm gettin' money, I don't get mad, ugh... Ask a nigga in my hood, Ask a nigga in my hood, he gon' say that I'm stamped... And when them situations came, I came out like a champ. When it was pourin' down rain and I came out of it damp.. But now it's champagne showers when we poppin' the champ', ugh"* I rapped along to the song while I speed through traffic.

I made it to the office in less than twenty minutes. Once inside, I headed straight to Harold's office to help him with his work.

"Thanks, son, for coming. You saved me big time. I don't know what I would do without you. You know I wanted to tell you that the promotion I had was yours. However, I couldn't do that with the drama your child mom was creating that would seem unfair. Your work ethic has been unmatched. It reminded me of myself when I was younger. You want this more than anything and don't let that fire die. 'Cause when you get to the top and get comfortable is when your problems will arise, never get comfortable." He schooled me while I began my work.

"I understand, there's no rush really as long as the position is held for me and only me. I always wanted to thank you for the opportunity and looking past my juvenile problems. Unlike other businesses, you didn't let my past define me." I replied.

"No need for that I saw something in you when you came in here for the position, and that same spark I saw hasn't left." He replied.

I nodded and silently did my work. I was on a roll, and by the time we were headed for lunch, we were more than halfway done. I even organized some of his business meetings for him. Sitting down in my office, I looked through some of my potential clients while eating the chicken wrap that I had ordered.

My cell phone rang, and my lawyer's name popped up, surprising me. I quickly answered, and he began to talk.

"So, I have some news for you, and it's not so great is now a good time to speak?" He questioned.

"Yeah, what's going on?" I asked while sitting my food down.

"Well, I received some news today. For one, you have a custody hearing as well as a hearing for increased child support. I thought I could easily get you shared custody and dismiss the increase of child support, seeing as though she just got an increase a few months ago. Now while that's still good, I may not be able to get the custody granted." Jackson informed me.

"Okay, so she is really bringing me to court for an increase and custody. How can I not win over her? She has no job. I'm the sole provider for Dream. I pay for her tutor, clothes and whatever else she needs, so how would I not be granted custody or even shared custody for the matter." I needed to know, Shay loved to play with fire and somehow the way my lawyer was speaking I was going to be the one to get burned.

"Now there is a way I can beat this for you, but before I make that type of commitment let me ask you this does Kamirra Mobley live with you?" Mr Jackson inquired.

"Yes, she's my fiancé. What does she have to do with Shay and me? She's not a part of this case." I replied.

"Well, DreQuan count your losses with this one, unless you

54

remove her from your home and can show proof by having her change her address and all. I'll send you over the video that Shay had her lawyer entered in as evidence of why your house wouldn't be good for Dream. This is also why you would lose this case before I could even fight it. I'll give you a week to touch back with me. Your hearing is scheduled for a month from now." He said before hanging up.

I stared at my computer screen, waiting for the email. Kamirra didn't even know it but whatever she did was going to have her homeless and sleeping from house to house if she hadn't saved that modeling money. I knew for a fact her overly religious mother wasn't going to allow her back into her home. Kamirra's mom was a church-going lady and didn't approve of anything Kamirra did.

Jackson's name appeared on the top of my screen, indicating that the email had been sent. I was nervous about opening it. As much as I wanted to see what the hell Kamirra did to have them saying she was the reason Dream couldn't be at my house. I also wanted to know what secret life she had been living that I didn't know of. My thoughts gave me the urge I needed to open the email. Once the video downloaded it, I made it big on the screen and pressed play.

Nothing seemed out of the ordinary, Mirra was in the bathroom standing in front of a mirror with a group of girls while the person recording held the phone through the small crack of a bathroom stall. The music blasting let me know that they were inside some kind of club and all the girls standing near Mirra were barely covered in the clothes they had on. I watched for about two minutes as they all took turns snorting lines off a mirror or something they were handing around. The entire time Mirra was fixing her makeup. One of the girls began dancing behind Kamirra and then whispered something into her ear. Kamirra smiled at her before turning to face her. They shared a quick kiss before Mirra took the mirror looking thing and snorted a line and then she did another before handing it back.

She held her head back for a minute and then began to dance. I watched the ten-minute video, and Kamirra snorted once more before they lit up some weed and smoked. The person who was recording finally stepped out of the stall and walked over to the sink. At that moment I noticed that Shay was the one who was recording. She smirked at Kamirra, waved at her and walked out, ending the video.

I clicked off the video and grabbed my food through it in the trash. I calmly walked to Mr. Harold's office.

"Hey, I know you needed me to stay; however, I have an emergency that came up dealing with my daughter and her mother. I don't want anything to be brought into the office so I figured I'd go handle it outside of the office. I'll come in early tomorrow morning, and finish up some more for you since I went through some of my potential clients already." I told him.

"It's okay, handle your business I appreciate all that you did do, and since we were almost done anyway, I don't need you coming in early. I should be able to finish up the rest today. I hope all is well." He told me.

"Thanks, see you tomorrow," I said before heading out.

I damn near ran out of the office and to my car. It was pouring down rain, and I still drove over the speed limit home. I was pissed, I asked this girl, and she lied to me. One thing I hated was a liar, and I was about to make good on my promise. I had to pray a few times and ask God not to allow me to put hands on her.

Pulling into my driveway, I hopped out of my car and jogged you the steps. I opened the door and looked around for Kamirra. Downstairs was empty looking, and I quickly remembered I paid for her modeling classes, and that was where she was supposed to be. I plopped down on the couch and dialed her phone number to see where she was at and what time she would be back. Just then, I heard her phone ring upstairs. I almost thought she left it home until she picked up.

"Hello." She said, sounding as if she was still asleep.

Instead of replying, I hung up the phone and flew up the steps heading straight to our bedroom.

"Get the fuck up now," I yelled, snatching the blanket off her naked body.

"What the hell is wrong with you Dre. Damn, I know I missed that class you paid for but it ain't that serious that little thousand dollars ain't hurt your pockets like that." She yawned.

"Bitch, if you don't get up I'm gone flip this fucking bed, now try me," I told her.

She quickly sat up and pulled my shirt over her head.

"Bitch? Oh, now I'm a bitch ? Your mother is the bitch." She yelled back stepping into my face.

"On my daughter, you better back your ass up before I break your fucking neck, or better yet your nose so you can't sniff shit else up it. I asked you was you snorting that shit AGAIN, and I asked you was there anything you could be doing to risk my fucking daughter being here and you lied to me. I gave you everything. I even allowed you to find a way to make money doing some shit I hated. You out here doing drugs and kissing these bitches who doing only God knows what. I took you from your mom's house and put you up in a fucking house. I brought you around my child, thinking you could possibly be someone she looked up to one day. I wanted you to be the mother to my next child. You had your little moment before, and I helped you get clean, and welcomed you back with open arms. I get that your dad was hooked on that shit and left it around, but you knew better than to try it. You saw first hand what it did to your pops. I mean I know some days I doubted our shit, and I even cheated a few times before and hurt you but I been on a straight path the last year and some change. And you do this to me?" I said as my voice cracked.

I felt my anger building up with the tears that filled my eyes. I wanted to cry not because she was doing drugs but because she hurt me, and at the same time gave another person the chance to have one up on me. I could lose my child behind this, and I knew Shay would hold it over my head if she won custody and not let me see my child.

"I'm sorry okay, it was supposed to be a one-time thing but then I just got addicted to it. I liked how it made me feel. Shit, you was so focused on work and Dream that I had to make fun with what I could and it just so happened to be a drug. Yes, I kiss girls here and there, but that's it. I didn't tell you cause you would judge me. Your dad was a crackhead, and he snorted shit too you, loved him and never switched up on him. How dare you stand there looking at me like I'm the nastiest bitch in the world." She said.

"Man, get the fuck out. We are done. I don't want shit to do with you, you need to have your address changed as well don't have no more mail sent here. Keep the ring and pawn that shit you might need the money. I'm taking you off my accounts before you can even make it to the bank to get money. I hope that you make it far with this modeling shit and don't let that drug habit get the best of you. I can't risk custody of my child because of you. I love you, but I love Dream way more. Now I can help you move this shit, or you can call one of your people to help, but it needs to be gone today while I'm home. Whatever you don't take is going in the trash." I replied, ignoring her comment about my grandma.

"I ain't doing shit, this my house as well as yours. And it's okay if you can't see Dream for a while, I'll go to rehab again. Just like last time, I'll come back clean and better than ever. Then they can let her come back. Why do you have to put me out to see her? You gone do that, choose her spoiled little ass over me? Your momma even did some drugs back in the day. She even sucked dick for it a few times just like her mom, and you love them bitches to death. I never heard you put her out of the house you pay for, but you can put me out?" She pushed me, causing me to take a step back.

"Don't put your hands on me and yeah my mom did, but she still made sure she ain't risk her kids or do that shit in front of us. My grandmom died doing that shit that was a lesson for my mom to quit. Stop speaking on my peoples cause I ain't speaking on yours. Now get your shit and go, I don't have time to play with you. The faster you bounce, the faster I can fix shit." I stepped out of her way once more.

She swung again this time connecting with my jaw. Instead of hitting her, I punched the wall leaving a big hole.

"Arghh," I yelled out in anger.

Kamirra must have taken me not hitting her back as a sign she could beat on me. She grabbed my shirt and began to swing wildly, hitting me anywhere she could. I grabbed her hands and slammed her against the wall. It was taking everything in me not to throw her out of the window or better yet off the balcony.

"Get your shit and go, the next time you hit me I'm hitting your ass back, and if you think about making me have to find you to change your address I'll make sure I have my little cousin make it easier for me and have your next address at a cemetery, or in your mother's China cabinet next to your perverted as daddy, your understand me." I threatened her.

"Yes. Let me go." She cried.

I let her go and took two steps back. She began to grab her things and take them to her car. I watched her until she had everything that was hers out of the house. I walked her to the door and stuck my hand out for my keys to my house. She could keep the car as it was a gift to her.

"I'm sorry." She said while wiping her tears.

"Yeah me too." I frowned slamming the door in her face, breaking my heart, and ending that chapter of my life.

❧ 9 ❧
LEAH

"**G**et the fuck up now." My mom yelled as she snatched the blanket off of me.

"Mom, just leave me alone," I whined, pulling the blanket back over my head.

"No, damn it. This is the third day in the row you have been laid up in this bed, and if you don't pull yourself together, you are going to be fired. I'm done catering to your damn kids as well, I love my grands, but my kids are grown. You are going to be late for work if you don't start moving now." My mom told me.

"I'm getting up damn." I sighed, sitting up.

I climbed out of bed and walked into the bathroom. I frowned at the ring that was left inside the tub and knew that came from my cousin Latrice and her filthy ass. She always took baths but never cleaned the tub after herself. I looked at the mousetrap behind the toilet and sighed. I loved my mother, but her house wasn't the best. She herself wasn't dirty, but the people she allowed to stay with her were. I couldn't see myself staying here for too long so I knew that I would have to save every paycheck until I got enough for a down payment on an apartment.

After turning on my music, I sat my phone on the counter. I grabbed the cleaning supplies off the shelf and began to clean the entire bathroom. I found myself crying and scrubbing the tub as *I wish I wasn't* by a Heather Headley played through the speakers.

"*Why you want to hurt me so bad? I believed in you, that's why I'm so mad. Now I'm drowning in disappointment, and it's hard for me to even look at you.*" I sang along with the song.

The salt from my tears made me scrub harder. I felt just like her. I wasted my time thinking this man was going to change. Yet, he never did. It took all of thirty minutes to complete my shower and wash my head. Now I didn't have that really good hair that shit you wet and curl up, so I had to spend another half an hour in the bathroom blowing drying it out until it was a big Afro.

I slid into my scrubs and then headed back to the room I was sharing with my kids. I looked around at the lil Romeo and T.I pictures that still hung on the wall from when I was a kid. The full-size bed was even still in the room with the pink and purple princess headboard. I had come from a four-bedroom home back to the same projects I ran from.

I sat down in front of my old vanity and placed my hair in two braids. I didn't bother with any makeup or anything else. Looking in the mirror, I saw a reflection of what I felt. A broken, lost girl. I was feeling like the same little girl who used to look in this same mirror wishing for love or just to feel like she was somebody. Wiping the silent tears away, I kissed my kids good-bye. Grabbing my wallet and my car keys, I headed for the front door.

"I couldn't wait to see you bitch." My cousin Shermaine called from her stoop looking dirty like she always did.

Instead of having a comeback, I continued to walk the short distance to my car. She had a lot more shit to be worried about like the eviction notice on her door.

"Bitch back like she never left. I guess your husband finally couldn't hide his shit no more or did he get tired of your ass and put you out?" She pressed.

Her ranting made the short walk seem so much longer. Still, I ignored her and continued on. Once I was inside my car I slammed the door shut and sat there. I felt like a bitch for letting her talk shit to me. However, had I responded I would have broken down and let her see just how hurt I really was, and I would never allow her to have that over me.

Driving to work, I decided against music. Letting down the windows, I welcomed the cool spring breeze. My phone rang, and I looked down at it. Nymir's name flashed across the screen and I wanted to throw it out the window. Not being as strong as I wanted to, I answered and listened to him.

"Baby, I've been calling you since you left. I'm sorry, I want you home with my kids. I'll put her out. Please, she's nasty as hell, and these damn babies don't listen. I miss you, I miss your cooking, I miss holding you at night. I promise I'll do right by our marriage please." He begged.

"You don't mean that, stop lying to me. You fucked up. I'm tired of fucking talking to you, it's getting old. You've done the most you can do, you hurt me for the last time. I don't want to fix nothing so stop asking me. The only thing we need to discuss is these kids, I need help with them. That's all, we don't have anything else to work out or anything." I snapped on the verge of tears.

"If you don't take me back, then what am I supposed to do? It's always been us against the world. You never let anything else break us apart. I told her to get rid of them kids. You forgave me for everything else to the point you didn't even care if I was cheating. You didn't say anything, so I thought it was cool. Yes, it was wrong, but you acted like it didn't faze you. You never believed anybody but me, so why change up on me now? You made me this way cause you allowed it. I miss my kids, can I at least get them for the weekend. I'll drop them off to school on

Monday, and we can go from there. I'll start by showing you I'm a good father. Then maybe we can work on our family again." He pleaded.

"I'll drop them off Friday, we don't have to exchange words." I hung up.

I pulled into a parking spot and sat in my car just for a while. Was it my fault that he'd cheated and made kids? Did I make him that way by ignoring all the signs and people? Was I as naive as he made it sound because I didn't go looking after a while? I knew he was creeping around. Too many people had the same stories. However, I never cared unless it was brought to me. My older cousins taught me at a young age, all men cheated. It was the ones who respected you enough not to bring it home that was forgivable. So when his shit started to come home, it was already too late. I was madly in love and on my way to being his wife. Then once I became the mother of his kids and wife, I started to care but shit I was the one he came home to. I was the one in the house with the ring and everything else. None of that mattered though, and maybe I was the one who was looking the most stupid. They all could leave, and he didn't owe them bitches a thing it was me who deserved the world, not them.

Getting out of my car, I placed my phone on silent. I stepped into work and went straight to the front desk. Usually, I would go in the break room and talk until my shift started, but I wasn't in a talking mood. Sitting at the check-in desk, I began my work. I checked in patients and stayed silent. Looking down at my finger, I stared at my ring.

"Excuse me, ma'am." A lady broke me from my thoughts.

"I'm sorry, how may I help you?" I questioned while sliding my ring off my finger.

"I just wanted to check in that's all." She smiled.

"Okay." I politely responded.

I began the work to check her in and updated her charts for her.

"Hey, when there's a God anything is possible. Keep your

head up. Things may seem dark now, but there's always a light at the end of the tunnel. You are beautiful, smile it'll help." She said before walking away.

I nodded my head at her and gave her a soft, weak smile. Those words she spoke to me touched me differently. I felt my eyes water, but I knew I couldn't cry right now. Hell, all I wanted to do is stop crying so I could focus on that light at the end of the tunnel. And as much as I wanted to, I felt like my troubles were just beginning. My left eye kept jumping, and my mother always told me when the left eye jumped trouble was coming to either a close friend or me.

After my eight-hour shift at work with no lunch break was over. I made my way right back to my mother's house. I climbed inside of my bed with my work clothes on and laid next to my kids.

"I cooked, I know you ain't eat since you forgot your debit card here with me. And you ain't take no lunch out for work." My mom said while sitting on the edge of my bed.

"I'm not hungry." I sighed.

"Okay, but you have to eat. You can't take care of them babies to your full ability if you ain't taking care of yourself." My mom said before walking out.

Running my hand over my face, I was quite tired of her. I knew everybody was just trying to help me, but nobody understood how hard this was for me. That man was my everything. We built everything together, and while he was still up, I was down. The one person I looked at like a friend, who I co-signed so she could keep her kids out of DHS and even when they took them I'm brought them into my home and raised them until she got herself together was the same female that couldn't tell me those were my husband kids.

I felt like a failure, I failed myself and most importantly, my kids. I didn't feel like I was good enough, and it was hard for me to push myself through this. How could I talk to them and tell them when all they would say is its just a man. There are plenty more out there. I wasn't even thirty,, and I had to go through the process of a divorce. My life felt like it had come to a complete stop and I wasn't sure how I was going to start it up again.

❧ 10 ❧

DRE

"I need to get my fucking social security card and birth certificate from your house," Kamirra yelled through the phone.

"I told you I wasn't home, and when I did get home, I would call you so you could come get it," I told her for the third time today.

"Dre, I'm not waiting for you to do whatever you have to do. That could take all day. You out shopping with your mom. I know how y'all trips like that go. I need my shit now. And if you don't have it, I'll call my cousins or some of my friends and have them kick your shit in." She screamed into my ear.

I let out a small chuckle, this girl was dying to get a taste of the person I left behind years ago. She was pushing buttons I didn't even know I still had.

"Go ahead and do what you go to do, just remember you gone get you and whoever the fuck you send hurt behind your bill shit. Now either get the shit when I get home or I can drop it by your moms. Either way it goes, stop fucking blowing my phone up." I replied right before I hung the phone up.

"What is she saying ?" My mom questioned soon as I slid my phone in my pocket.

66

"That shit doesn't even matter. I just know if she makes good on any of that hot shit she was speaking I'm putting lil cuz on her head and that's a promise." I snarled.

"She's just upset and talking like that because of it." My mom tried to reason.

Ignoring what she said I picked up some oranges for Dream, it was both of our favorite fruits. Maybe Kamirra was upset, and she had a right to be. However, that had nothing to do with me anymore. She should have known that it would be over once I found out what she was doing. To make matters worse, she knew that she could put my child and at my shared custody at risk, and she did it anyway.

"Besides that's how have you been doing son? I heard you were almost the owner of that promotion you were working for. What happened to that?" My mom asked while looking through fruits.

"It should have been mine, Shay's ass kept popping up and doing all that dramatic shit she does. On everything I love, I feel like those two bit-." I went to say but was cut off.

"Now don't even play with me like that. Regardless of how you feel about them you won't call them bitches in my presence." My mom scolded.

Carmen was as sweet as they came. However, she was raised on respect and would knock me upside the head anytime I got disrespectful with any elderly people or females. She was all of five foot, and at forty-five, she still looked and could run with the best of them. My mom kept herself together and was big on health. She worked in and out of hotels my entire life, and I felt like she wouldn't quit until they fired her.

I was the spitting image of my mom and what you could call a mama's boy. We had a strong bond, and she always blamed it on having me while she was still young herself. Carmen's dark chocolate skin was wrinkle-free, She had the same jet black curly hair as me, and while I had one deep dimple, she had two.

"Boy, you really are not gone talk to me if I get my ass done.

All my life I had these big ass boobs with a flat butt. I mean it's not flat-flat, but it ain't out there. I had my fair share of doing some of everything that I ain't too proud of. I'm damn near fifty I need to finally get me a man worth marrying." My mom said, breaking me from my thoughts.

"How did we go from my problems to you getting your butt done?" I frowned at her.

"You took too long to respond to me. Keep zoning out and shit. When you go get Dreamy? I want to take her with me to the salon." She asked me.

My mom was the queen at switching subjects, she could never stay on one for too long.

"I told you I'm supposed to get her tonight. I ain't even gone lie I think Shay gone do something so that I can't get her and if she does I'm gone be sick. She knows how I feel about my daughter and the best thing she can do to hurt me is to keep her away from me. I feel like I just keep repeating the same shit every chance I get. I'm tired of it, now when I become one of them niggas who don't care and just let the courts handle it and stop all the other shit she gone be mad. I'm telling you, she will be homeless if she keeps it up. I ain't got to pay a mortgage, rent, or anything of that matter." I said, getting angry.

"Everything happens for a reason, you are strong. You've been through some shit to get where you at, and you don't let no bitch or nigga take you back to where you came from. You made it out, baby, so don't go flashing back because of some shit that's out of your control. All you can do is continue to be the man I taught you to be. Continue to be the father Dream needs you to be. She's all that matters until you find you a wife. Now I liked Shay when y'all were younger. She was the perfect match for your crazy. You ain't that person no more, and I admit at first I didn't see what you were saying about her and I figured that you just got big-headed once you graduated college. I didn't realize that it was just you turning into the young man you needed to become. At that moment, I decided you knew how to make the best decisions for your life, and you were on to the right path. I said all that to say this, don't let one little mishap ruin something you worked your whole life to create." My mom said while we stood in the middle of the market.

"Heard you." We got our things, and I paid for them.

We walked out of the market, and I placed everything in the trunk while she stood on the side and talked on the phone. Once I had everything in the car I helped my mom in, I jogged around the car and climbed in. Turning up the music, I nodded my head to the beat. Instead of dropping my mom home first, I went by Shay house to grab Dream since they lived close, and my mom was cooking on the grill. I threw my car in park and climbed out. I knocked on the door until I got an answer.

"Dream ain't home, she is with my mother. I tried to call you, but you didn't answer. I told her to call you cause she wanted to spend the weekend with her." She shrugged.

"You knew I was supposed to get her, you on your shit. I been calling you and you ain't answer you know it's my weekend it's been my weekend for at least two years now," I replied.

Shay was known to do this anytime shit ain't go her way. Since we had the courts involved, she had been following their orders for the most part.

"Well, she ain't here, so you have to try again next weekend." She laughed slamming the door in my face.

I stood there for a second, just looking at the door. I raised my foot to kick that muthafucka down.

"You better not, god gone handle that for you." My mom yelled from the car.

Putting my foot down, I walked away in defeat. Everybody was always telling me to be the bigger person yet that shit wasn't getting me nowhere.

"I don't know how much longer I can do the right thing. I just want to be the perfect dad to my daughter. I'm trying to be the best man I can fucking be or know how to be to her, and this bitch keeps playing with me. Like I'm a fucking sucker, ain't nobody ever disrespect me this much." I snapped slamming my car door shut.

I sped off in the direction of my mother's house while she yelled out all kinds of profanity and prayers for us to make it to her home safely. I tuned her completely out and thought of what was next. Playing nice wasn't getting me ahead, so I was going to fight fire with fire from here on out.

𝕝 II 𝕝

LEAH

M onday had come and gone, and I tried calling Nymir for
the fifth time in a row, yet all my calls went unanswered.
This was one of the reasons I didn't want him to take the kids;
however, I didn't want to seem like a bitter mom nor wife and
not allow him to see his kids. I don't know whether they hadn't
made it to school, nor did he even reach out to me and tell me
that he would drop them off home. I was sitting outside of
Cion's school, contemplating if I should drive to his house and
see if he was there or back to my moms to wait on him.

"Nymir, it's me again. I know you see me calling, please pick
up and let me speak to the kids. I also need to know when you
are bringing them home or if you want me to meet you so that I
can get them. Please call me back." I left a voicemail.

Saying fuck it, I drove to his house and rung the bell a few
times only to receive no answer. I began to bang just because I
saw Morgan's car in the driveway. Minutes later, she swung the
door open. She stood before me in a T-shirt looking like I had
woken her up.

"Hey, umm, Nymir isn't here. He left with the kids this
morning and haven't been back since." She said while trying to
fix her hair.

"Do you know if he is going to bring them home or where they went?" It pained me to ask her.

"No, and I didn't get a chance to apologize to you, I know I fucked up, and I owe you at least that." She started, but I turned to walk away. An apology from her was something I could give one fuck about.

"Look if it helps, I heard him telling his mom that he didn't plan on giving them back to you." She yelled, causing me to turn around and look at her.

"What? He said what?" I questioned storming back over to her.

"Look I don't want any trouble." She placed her hands in the air.

"What did you say?" I asked her again.

"He said he was going to keep them, he wasn't going to give them back to you. Something about a conversation y'all had. He told her that you wouldn't agree to let him see the kids your sister had to force you. He said you had been keeping them away from him and he's been begging since you left to see them. He wanted you to hurt like you was hurting him. I'm not sure how true it is but that's what he's telling his family." She spilled.

"Are you fucking serious?" I yelled out to no one in particular.

Running back to my car, I headed over to his mom's house and got no answer from her she didn't even pick up the phone. Doing the next best thing, I headed back to my mom's house so that I could get pictures of them. I was going to wait and see if he would answer me and if not I would get the police involved. I got on my knees on the side of my bed and closed my eyes.

"God, if you hear me right now please God, don't let him keep my babies from me. God, please allow them to return back to me. I know he has the house and I don't. However, I'm their mom and the best parent to them I could be. Oh, God, please help me. I'm trying to do the best I can while handle everything the best I can please God, please don't let him take my babies from me." I cried while praying to God.

The knock on the door made me sit down on my ass and try and wipe my tears away.

"Hey, babe. Where are the kids?" Amelia asked.

"Their dad has them." I responded.

"Perfect get your ass up and dressed we going out tonight mama." She smiled.

"No, I can't it's a school night I need to wait for my babies," I said.

"What they with they daddy, they gone be fine come on you gotta get the hell out this dark ass room. Put on some cute shit get dolled up, so you feel good and go grab some other nigga's attention. You'll forget about that loser in no time." She said.

"Fuckkkkk, just leave me the fuck alone please," I screamed out in frustration.

"What the hell?" Amelia frowned at me.

"Look I don't want to go out okay, I need to wait here. Morgan told me that Nymir plans on keeping my kids from me. He called me before I gave them to him and asked me to come back home. I told him no, and then he asked to see his kids. I agreed for him to get them Friday. I didn't want to be a bad parent and keep them away from him. Had I known he was up to this I would have never agreed to this shit. Why did he want to do this to me, he's hurt me enough. I can barely think straight, and he pulls this? I just wanna get right Mi. I want to do right by my kids, seeing them every day was what kept me fighting. I know I been down, but they are the only thing that can keep me up. What I'm gone do, man?" I finally let go of the tears I had been holding in fall.

"Listen, you keep fighting. Mommy ain't raise no bitches. We are strong, and there's always a way. Even if you have to go to court with him, you'll be able to see them. If worse comes to worst, they will give you visitations. You use that time to build yourself up. Show him you can get on your shit without him. You have the job already. He doesn't know shit about them. However, don't make things harder on yourself. Take him to court and even if they go with him for a while be the one who comes out on top. Get your shit together, you can still have fun. Live your life, you are not tied down anymore." My sister said while sitting on the floor with me.

She rubbed my hair while I cried into her shirt, soaking it with tears and snot. My phone rings, making me jump and pull away from her. My heartbeat sped up when I read Nymir on the screen. My shaky hands almost made it impossible to answer, but I did.

"Hello," I said.

"Are you coming home yet?" He questioned, though I couldn't see him I knew he had his signature smirk on his face.

"No, are you bringing the kids home? Please don't keep them from me." I cried. I knew Amelia had just told me to be strong yet I couldn't find it in me.

"They are home, you're the one not home. Do what you have to do, call the cops if you want. You have no custody of them, and neither do I. They're at home enjoying their games and dolls, they don't want to go back to that roach-infested, project base shelter your mom is running." He spat into the phone.

"Okay, I'll be there with the police soon." I sighed before hanging up.

I looked over at my sister, and for the first time, she kept her mouth shut as I slid my feet into a pair of PINK slides. She stood up and walked out the door behind me. I called the police and had them meet me at Nymir's house. The fifteen-minute ride felt like hours due to the silence and the thoughts that filled my head. We pulled up, and I was about to jump out until Amelia grabbed my hand.

"Listen whatever happens I have your back. You are strong, and your time to shine will come." She offered a soft smile.

Nodding my head, I got out of the car. I walked over to the police and began to explain what had happened.

"Alright, there is honestly nothing we can do. We have talked to the kids, and they want to stay here. This is something you two have to take to court. My advice to you always make sure you have custody. If you don't, we can't rightfully remove them from the other parent unless there are signs of neglect or abuse, in this case, it isn't any." The officer let me know.

I looked over at Nymir, and he opened the door as if he was welcoming me in. Turning back to the cop, I asked.

"Could you at least get them so that I can see them, please. It's been days since I have seen them and he only let me talk to them the other day. Please, I just want to hug them and tell them I love them. I won't try anything else." I sobbed.

The officer walked over to Nymir and got the kids. I smiled and ran over to them once they were close to me. I pulled them both into a hug and kissed their face one by one.

"Come on mom that's nasty." Cion smiled, wiping my kids off his cheek.

"Don't play with me. I love y'all, make sure you call me from your iPad. I miss y'all so much. Whenever y'all want to come back to mom's house with me, just let me know." I said.

"Mommy, don't cry." Callie frowned while wiping my tears.

"I'm sorry baby," I said, trying to suck it up. However, my tears just kept falling.

After a few minutes, the officer walked the kids back to Nymir, and I got in my sister's car. I laid my head back in the seat, wondering how I got here. I had to get my life in order and fast. There was no way I would allow him to raise my kids and keep them from me.

❧ 12 ❧

DRE

The month had come and gone June was hotter than a bitch, and the clubs had been lit. Yet, the summer wasn't the same for me. Each summer, I got my daughter from July until the weekend before school started back up. Instead, here I was sitting on this funky ass trolley on my way to court. I could have driven, but I didn't want to drive downtown. Parking was always hard to find. The good thing was I worked downtown so the trolley ride wouldn't be that long.

I was seated next to this pretty brown skin girl. Her hair was in a bushy puffball that looked like she tried to make it look neat. Even with the slight bags under her eyes, she looked beautiful. Here and there she would look down at her phone at two kids. One looked exactly like her, while the other had her same colored skin. She also would look at me through the mirror, and when we would connect eyes, she would look back down.

"Excuse me, do you know which stop is for the courthouse," I asked her, even though I knew.

She quickly lifted her head at the sound of my voice and turned to face me. Her mouth was left slightly opened as if she was star struck. Just then, I saw how beautiful she really was. I had to bite the corner of my lip to keep from expressing how I really felt. What I wanted to tell her was that if she kept her mouth opened like that, I could definitely place something in it.

"Umm, it depends on which court you're going to." She said, clearing her throat.

"I need to go to the one for custody of a child," I replied, licking my lips.

"That's the fifteenth street stop, it's the next stop." She said just above a whisper.

"Thank you beautiful." I smiled.

She smiled back at me, showing all thirty-two of her pretty white teeth. I knew if she was any lighter, her cheeks would be red from blushing. She wiped a loose strand of hair out of her face before looking back down at her phone. The trolley had started to move, and she pulled the string. When she stood up, my mouth was the one to drop this time. I could tell from her figure with her sitting down that she would have either a nice ass or just some nice hips and thighs. However, when she stood up, her chunky ass was on full display, making my mouth water.

"Excuse me." She said lowly.

I stood up and made my way over to the door since this would be my stop too. Once the trolley stopped, I stepped off and walked up the steps. I was wishing I gave her my number or even my business card, yet time wasn't on my side for me to stop and turn back. I jogged up the steps after checking my watch and realizing that I had about three minutes to make it. Instead of taking in the city like I usually did when I had court, I was power walking to the building.

Once inside of the courthouse, I went up to floor six and patiently waited for my case to be called. Shay was in the waiting area over in a corner talking with her lawyer. This would be just like her, the bitch was late for everything but as soon as it was a court date she was always early. She was rocking an all-white business suit paired with some silver, red bottoms. For her to be struggling, she sure wasn't dressed like it. Her hair was in a long weave with a part in the middle. I couldn't lie, she looked good as hell. However, I wouldn't fuck her with a ten-foot pole.

"Daddy." Dream yelled as she ran over to me.

I turned and looked at my little baby. It had felt like years since I last saw her though it had only been a few weeks. I got down on one knee and let her wrap her arms around me.

"I missed you Dreamy," I told her.

"I missed you too, why haven't you come to get me? Mommy said it's because Mirra is sick that you can't come. That's why we had to come here today, is Mirra okay? ." Dream questioned me.

"She's okay, and we have to come here so that maybe mommy and I can get better with our parenting when it comes to you. Sometimes we have to do that so we can make sure you get what's best for you. What have you been up to? Have you taken any trips so far? Are you enjoying your summer?" I asked question after question.

"I haven't been anywhere yet, I have to go to summer camp now because mommy said she needs her time. I hate summer school. It's hot in there, and we don't do anything fun. I wish I could come with you like we used to do." She whined.

"Me too, and hopefully the judge okay's it." I smiled at her.

Shay looked over at us and frowned. She got up, and I knew she was about to walk over and start some shit. Standing up to my full height, I easily towered over them both.

"Dream, come over here and sit down. You know better than to be running in this place screaming." Shay scolded her.

"I'm sorry, mommy." Dream apologized while holding on to my leg.

"If you would let me see her, then she wouldn't have to act like that when she sees me," I said in anger.

"If the judges say you can have her, then that's what we gone do. Until I get what I asked for you won't get what you're asking for. Now we could have done this my way and not be here. Buttttt, you wanna let your little snorty mama tell me what I can and can't do. See how she did all that and now she's hopefully gone, and Dream is gone from you too." She laughed.

I could have smacked the smile off her face. Instead, I looked at my daughter and continued playing with her. Shay was starting to make me hate her more than I already did and if my daughter wouldn't have been so heartbroken, I would have had my little cousin make her a distant memory.

"So you gonna ignore me?" She tapped my shoulder until I looked at her.

"Man, why you can't just let me be happy. I don't fuck with you. I take care of my daughter, and I do what I'm supposed to as a man. No matter what you have a roof over your head and I'm not even sure if you still work anymore or just living off my daughter. This is not going to be some shit you just feel like you can keep doing. I'm getting tired of this and you. I'm really doing my best to keep on; however I'm ready to become one of them nigga who don't do shit for they kids at all. You really pushing me Shay to be that way." I told her honestly.

"I let you be happy, you were happy with me at one point, and then you got you some money, and your taste in women and their behavior changed. We were one big family, you forgot you were just as ratchet as me back in the day. We fought together, hustled together, cried together, and everything else. Yet, you always try and downplay what we had like you ain't love me. You broke my heart and moved on so I'm gone make you feel the hurt I felt anyway I can. Then you go get you a girl and try and give her all the things we made plans on. How did she get a ring before me? I'm not even jealous, which is crazy. I'm more so hurt you couldn't accept my ratchet ways, but you accepted her drug habits. I watched the man I loved my whole life love someone else more than me. And yeah I cheated but so did you." She said on the verge of tears.

Just as I went to respond to her, they called our case. Shay quickly wiped her eyes and walked in the direction of the courtroom. I held onto Dream's hand, and we followed close behind her. Yeah, I left Shay, but it was just because as we grew older, our visions for life were completely different. I wanted out of the hood while she wanted to stay in it. I wanted the house with the white picket fence, and she wanted hers right smack in the middle of the hood. She was fine with Tasker projects especially once they fixed them up. She wanted to have the best apartment in the whole project complex while I wanted desperately to get away from them. It took me years to convince her to let me help her buy a house away from there so she could raise my daughter in a better environment.

"So we are asking for an increase in child support. Can we explain what for?" The judge asked.

"Yes, my client has asked for it to be raised due to her losing her job, as well as the child now attending summer camp, and activities for the summer." Shay's lawyer said while reading from her paper.

"And you don't agree with this, why?" The judge directed her question to me.

"Well because your honor, I already pay her mortgage in full, as well as any needs such as clothes, shoes, down to hair supplies, or things Dream wants to do. We also just had a raise a few months back for tutoring which Dream has never received. I feel like at this point I'm just giving her money for unknown reasons." I replied.

"Dream is an honor roll student, so why would she still need a tutor?" Shay yelled.

"She's been on honor roll since she started school so if she doesn't need one now why did she need one then? And she told me she has never had a tutor, as well as I have paperwork from her school stating she has never had nor did she ever need one." I shot back.

"Enough, I'll ask a question, and you will answer. You two don't need to speak to each other because if you could, we wouldn't be here. Now, as far as child support goes I will not be giving you a raise, I see no reason. I also will drop the price back down because it seems as if the child doesn't need the tutor based on what you both just said. Now usually I don't do your custody case but today I will. I can see that there are claims of a drug addict in a home, which is why Nashay here doesn't feel comfortable with the child being in the home of the father. She also submitted a video with evidence." Judge Hanks said.

"Yes ma'am, the addict, in this case, has been removed from my clients home. He had no knowledge of this going on as it was never done in the home. He reported to me that as soon as he got wind of what was going on, he broke things off and had her leave the home. Which is why we would like to keep the partial custody as it was already set." My lawyer spoke.

"Your honor, this lady and based on the video, you can see is a frequent drug user. She is the fiancé of this man and has lived with him for years. She still uses the address and claims to live there. I can show you she has said this via text messages to my client. We would like to ask you to allow Nashay to have full custody just until we can prove that this lady is no longer in the home with the father." Shay's lawyer went up to the judge and gave her printed pictures of I'm guessing text messages.

My lawyer went up to view the evidence as well. When he turned around, I could see on his face the outcome of this. My heart rate increased, and it felt like I would have a heart attack once the judge set the papers down and looked at me.

"I'll be giving you thirty days to turn in a copy of her Id without your address on it. Or some proof that she has indeed moved out. Until then, Dream is to remain in the custody of her mother. Case dismissed." She banged her gavel.

I could have passed out when she said that. While Shay walked out of the courtroom with a smile on her face, I had to sit down and gather myself. At this point, I couldn't hold the tears from falling. I knew that Kamirra was going to give me hell to get her address changed, but I was willing to do anything to have my way.

"Hey man, we can get through this, this is something minor.

And it's not permanent so hold it together. I know you miss her and she misses you too. You'll be back together in no time." Jackson patted my back.

"Thanks, man." I wiped my tears and stood up.

With my head down, I walked out of the courthouse and into the pouring rain. I guess God knew how I felt because as soon as I saw Dream getting into a car with her mom, she must have seen me too. She waved goodbye as the car pulled off, and my tears fell. The rain helped disguise them. I walked down to the train station and reached in my pocket for my wallet only for it to be gone. I searched my pockets again and came up empty-handed. Palming my face, I pulled out my phone and ordered an Uber home. I didn't even care to get my car from work. I would handle everything tomorrow. My life felt like it had come to a complete halt, and everything I worked hard for was gone in a matter of hours.

13

LEAH

Sitting in my car, I stared between the address on the gun license in my hand and at the door. My stomach turned and not in a bad way as I contemplated ringing the doorbell and handing him his wallet or just putting it in the mailbox. I really didn't want to put in the mailbox in case this was his old address. From the outside, the home looked beautiful. The two-story home was to die for on the outside. Saying fuck it, I got out of the car and rang the doorbell about four times only to get no answer. There was a car in the driveway, so I knew somebody was home. At that moment, I opted to put the wallet in the mailbox. I didn't want it to be a lady that was there, and she tried to fight because of the fact I was returning her man's wallet. Just as I bent down to put it into the mailbox, the door swung open.

"I said, who the fuck is it?" He growled.

"Umm, I'm sorry to bother you, I just wanted to return this. You dropped it on the trolley, and I couldn't catch up to you once you got off." I stuttered, holding my hand out to give him his wallet.

I kept my eyes glued to his naked chest. This man went to the gym, and his strong arms told it all. I wondered if he worked out all the time and just exactly how much he bench-pressed crossed my mind. My panties grew wet at the thought of him lifting me so I could ride those juicy ass lips.

"Yo, you heard me?" He snapped his fingers in my face.

"Huh, no. What did you say?" I asked him.

"I said thank you and would you like to come in. I don't know you that well but from the looks of it you had a fucked up day and so did I, we could have a drink and talk. As two complete strangers, we can't take sides or judge too much cause we don't know the other people." He offered.

I had no plans on coming into this man's house, let alone having a conversation with him. If I did, I would have at least tried to make myself look more presentable. My hair was still in a messy ponytail, and my eyes I'm pretty sure were swollen from crying. I had on a pair of Nike tights and a white tank top with a pair of sandals.

"Never mind, you don't have to. I see the look on your face. I don't know what I was thinking. Can I pay you for bringing my wallet back?" He rambled while rubbing his waves.

"No, it's okay. I could use someone to talk to." I smiled, but on the inside, I was a nervous wreck.

"God, please protect me and allow me to come out of this alive at least, if not with a new friend and feeling better," I said a quick prayer in my head before walking in.

"Would you like anything to drink? I have some water, just about any alcohol you can think of, as well as juice, and Gatorade. I don't drink soda so none of that." He asked once he closed the door and locked it.

"Do you know how to make a mimosa? If so I'll take that and a bottle of water." I replied following behind him.

Just like I expected the inside of the house was beautiful and clean. I could tell a woman had either decorated or helped based on the black, yellow and white theme he had going on in the entire downstairs.

"You can sit down if you like or you can continue to follow

me. I'll bring everything for your drink and make it in front of you if that helps." He laughed.

"Okay," I spoke before having a seat on the leather couch.

From the couch, I was able to see a few pictures on the tv stand. Most were of him and females. There were very few of him and another male. The biggest picture was him and a little girl. She was beautiful, and he smiled so hard in the picture.

"That's my daughter Dream." He said scaring the shit out of me.

"Whoa, shit," I yelled out, clenching my chest.

"My bad, I ain't mean to scare you. I thought you heard me walk in. I brought closed bottles so you wouldn't think I was trying to slip you something." He set everything down on the table.

I watched him as he sat down and then made our drinks. He was so damn fine it didn't make any sense. I would love to meet his mother just to thank her for giving me something to look at.

"So, I'm DreQuan. Most people call me Dre. I'm a bank investor, and I'm twenty-eight years old. I have a seven-year-old daughter named Dream. What about you?" He started the conversation.

His voice was so smooth, and he licked his lips ever so often. I silently wished he licked me like I was his lips.

"I'm Aleah, most people call me Leah. I'm twenty-seven, I have a son Cion, and a daughter Callie. Cion is older, he's about to be seven and Callie is four. I am married, well I was married. I'm currently separated and about to start the process of a divorce and trying to get my shit together. I work at University hospital, and I am a patient service representative. That's about all there is to me." I sat back, taking a sip from the drink he handed me.

"So why were you crying? If you don't mind me asking. I invited you in cause you look like you had a long day. I could see even on the trolley you looked down. And from the looks of it, shit ain't get no better. I don't know if you want it or need it however maybe it will help, so my offer to pay you for returning my wallet is still open." Instead of him drinking from a cup, he picked up the bottle of Hennessy and drank from it. Letting me know he either had some problems too, or he was a functioning alcoholic.

"I did have a long day, it wasn't so good. This whole process is taking a toll on me as well as my kids. Right now, they have to bounce from house to house since I decided to leave. I took them to their fathers for the weekend trying to be a mother and not a bitter one, and he takes and keeps them pass Monday. I don't know what I was thinking I should have known he was up to something since he only asked after I told him I wasn't coming back home. Of course, the kids had no problem staying with him because that's been home to them their entire lives. Their rooms, games and all are there. "Now with me, we're all cooped up in one room. Until I save up enough to get my own place." The words flew from my mouth.

For some reason, I started off trying to be guarded; however, the more I talked, the more I opened up. I hadn't known this man a full twenty-four hours, and I felt like I could tell him everything. I was feeling like them girls in movies or books that just meet a guy and the same day giving him her whole life story. I guess this shit wasn't so unbelievable cause here I was doing the same shit I laughed at in books.

"I know that feeling a little. I haven't gone through a divorce, but recently I had to break things off with my fiancé. I thought she was the one. I thought we knew everything about each other. You know, we had no secrets, everything was out there. That's what she had me thinking. My baby mom is nothing like you if what you saying is true. I pay for her to have a home, child support and anything else my daughter needs however she always asks the courts for an increase. I told her I wasn't giving her no more money and she takes me to court and gives them a video of my fiancé snorting coke in a club bathroom. Mind you I asked the girl if there was anything she was doing that had my baby mom saying she was gone be the reason I don't see my daughter. This woman lied to me, had me finding out while I was at work. I put her out because I could accept that. We went to court today, and they didn't raise my child support; however, I have a month to prove she doesn't stay here anymore. This female had the nerve to text my baby mom and tell her she was still staying with her knowing she was gone to bring that up in court. I know it's gone be hard to get her to change her address and give me proof, but I got to do whatever I can. I love my daughter, and not seeing her is killing me." The way he spoke about his daughter played with my emotions and had me about to cry for him.

"Damn, maybe you should try asking her. Record a conversation with y'all stating she don't live here just in case you can't get what you need. At least you have something." I told him.

"You right, as far as you though, what's stopping you from getting your own place? I know a few people who own rental places as well as realtors. I could make a call for you. I mean I do owe you a favor since you haven't said anything about me paying you." Dre said while staring at me.

"Your money's no good over here. I did what I was supposed to do by returning it. And no thank you for the help, I would like to do that on my own once I'm ready. You don't owe me anything. Talking to me was enough, you helped me get things off my chest and feel better, and you didn't judge me not once." I winked at him.

"At least let me have your number since I can't repay you with money. I can at least be there when you need someone to talk to and vice versa." He said, and just like that, I rattled my number off to him.

I was feeling the mimosa and the conversation which is probably why I didn't notice I had already downed four cups. A crashing sound ended the peacefully quiet moment we were having, and Dre jumped up, grabbing a gun from underneath the couch and rushing to the door. Not knowing what was going on,

I grabbed my pocketbook and sat it on my lap. Reaching inside of it, I cocked my 9mm handgun and held it in my hand. Dre looked back and smiled at me before heading to the door.

"What the fuck is wrong with you? Huh, I told you you could come get your shit in the morning before I went to work. You out your fucking mind, you just threw a fucking brick in my window." I heard Dre yelling.

"Fuck you and that window. I told you I wanted my shit and my brother gone see to it that I get it. Beat his ass Gotti if he doesn't let me go up in there." She screamed.

"Ain't nobody beating my ass that's on my mom. You come around here drawing for what? You ain't coming in my house. I'll bring your shit to the door, and if you want some smoke nigga we can have it." Dre barked.

"What's up then, you trying to get bold with a gun in your hand put it down and fight like a man." I heard must have been the brother say.

"What did I get myself into?" I said just as a female came running in.

"Oh, see you got a bitch in here Dre? That's why I couldn't come." The girl yelled angrily.

She was pretty as hell. I watched her not saying nothing as she began her walk towards me. I pulled my hand from my bag and held on to my gun.

Dre came storming in the house with a male following behind him.

"See, now I'm gone, throw your ass out." He snatched the girl up by her shirt.

Everything after that happened quickly. The guy punched Dre in the face and Dre stumbled. He let go of the girl and swung back. Dre was throwing punches that connected every time while the guy swung wildly.

"This what the fuck you wanted? Huh." Dre questioned the girl.

He had her brother on the ground, one hand wrapped around

his neck while he repeatedly punched him with the other hand. It had to be the drinks because as fucked up as the situation was he looked good as hell beating that man's ass.

"Get off my brother." She ran over to Dre and swung.

He stood up and pushed her, making her fall over. His big abusive ass was looking like a different person than the man I originally came in and was talking to. This was not the sexy man in the suit but a thug from the hood in ball shorts with no shirt standing before me. Dre looked over at me, and I could have sworn I saw a flash of regret in his eyes.

He grabbed something in an envelope off the end table and threw it at the girl.

"Get the fuck out now. You wanted your shit right, you got it. Change your fucking address and stop lying to people like we still together and you live here. If you have anybody else pull up to my muthafucking house getting their ass beat ain't the only thing they gone get. Now take your weak ass brother and bounce bitch. And homie if you still want some more I got some hot shit that has your name on it. You should have come and asked why I put your sister out like a man. Try me again if you fucking want I'll have y'all whole family getting buried. Now get the fuck out before it be a double homicide in this bitch." Dre snapped.

The guy got up off the ground and nodded his head. The girl who I gathered was the fiancé at some point tried to run over to Dre, but the brother pulled her out the house. Dre slammed the door then walked back over as I stood up to leave.

"I apologize that you had to see that. I swear to God I don't usually have shit like that happening to me. I'm not gone say I'm not like that; however, I usually know how to keep my cool. Unfortunately, in this situation, I could not." He tried to explain.

"It's cool, I'm going to go ahead and head home. I have work in the morning, and it's pretty late, call me tomorrow maybe if you want to talk." I replied.

I placed my gun back inside my bag and walked over to the door. Dre followed me walking me all the way to my car.

"Please don't judge me from that shit. I ain't saying I'm a perfect nigga, but I am a man first. I don't take disrespect lightly. I'm gonna be holding you to that phone call too." He closed my car door, and I drove off.

Even though his ass was crazy, I was looking forward to that phone call the next day even though I wasn't sure if I would answer. The last thing I wanted was another toxic man in my life.

❧ 14 ❧
DRE

"**M**iss, this first thing I will need is your background and experiences. What's unique about your company and most importantly, what is your market size?" I repeated myself to the lady that sat in front of me.

"I told you already, I ain't got that much credit, but my hustle is real. My brand is unique it's called Hot Stuff cause I got all the hot stuff people looking for. I have bundles, clothes that are made by me and I'm working on candles. Here smell this one." She said, handing me a candle that smelt like ass.

"You should keep working on those smells." I handed it back to her.

"Seriously, where yo boss at. Because we are not bout to play. I sold about ten of these already to my granny, and she loved them. I need this shit, oouu excuse me. I need this to get started y'all say y'all can help anybody." She moved around in her seat like she had crabs.

"We just may not be able to help you. If we invest in you how likely are you to sell your bundles and other hot stuff? It's a lot of people selling these same things. What makes you better than them is what I'm asking." I replied.

I was growing frustrated, and between the nappy ass wig this lady came in wearing and her moving around with those funky ass candles I was sure my office smelled of ass and throw up. I didn't know who set her on my list, but I was going to find out and curse their ass out.

"You know what, maybe my boss can explain this better to you. Grab all your merchandise, and I can walk you right over to his office if you want." I smiled.

She jumped up and grabbed her suitcase full of shit, I almost lost my mind when a roach fell from the bag.

"Oh my God, was that a roach?" She screamed.

I did a double-take at her and bit my bottom lip before I could curse her ass out. I stepped on the roach before it could get under my desk. I quickly walked her to Mr. Harold office and rushed out, leaving him to deal with her and her roaches.

Back inside my office, I left the door open for it to air out and cleaned off my seat and desk. I was praying like hell she ain't have bed bugs the way she was moving around. Grabbing the Lysol can from my bathroom I sprayed the chair until it was soaking wet and I was coughing. I made a mental note to get some shit for roaches just in case some of them ran out that I didn't see.

"I ain't taking no more clients today, especially not anybody that doesn't send in their paperwork beforehand. I need to go home and shower." I told the receptionist.

Walking outside, I pulled my suit jacket off and shook it before placing it inside my trunk. I called Leah only for it to go to voicemail. I was starting to feel like that shit that happened with Kamirra had her scared of me and not wanting to talk until my phone dinged letting me know I had a text message.

Leah - At work, I will call you when I either take a break or done my shift.

I smiled at the simple text and got in my car. I wanted to ask her if I could pick her up after work. Hell, I would have been okay with pulling up just to walk her from the door to her car, just so I could be in her presence again. For some odd reason, she made me feel at ease. Though I would have loved to fuck her and see if that pussy was as good as she looked, I wanted to know her more.

The drive to my house was full of thoughts of her. I felt like a bitch just waiting on her to call me when she got off. I took my shower then headed to the courts to play ball with my cousins.

Kamirra called my phone, and I quickly denied the call. I knew putting her on the block list would only prompt her to call my job phone or call me from other numbers.

"Man, you had to shower to come play ball and get dirty again. What kind of shit is that?" Don joked.

"Fuck you, this bitch came in my job with roaches in her suitcase that shit had me creeped the fuck out. I went home washed the filth off of me cause you know dirt might be airborne. Then I threw my clothes in the trash I can't risk having no roaches man them shits is bad. Once I left Tasker, I promised I would do my house right so them roaches don't come for me." I frowned snatching the ball from him.

"Man, roaches were family to you at one point don't act like that." Joc, one of Don's friends said.

"Fuck both of y'all, that's why my house ain't connected to nobody's and gets a thorough cleaning once a week. Y'all like laying up in roach-infested places. If I even see one roach, I get paranoid, that makes me have anxiety." I said truthfully.

Growing up in the projects roaches were in every home and didn't care when they came out or crawled on you. As much as my mom kept the house clean, the roaches wouldn't leave. Even when the maintenance man came and sprayed whatever that spray was talking about "they gone come out, but they should die." They still didn't die.

"Pick y'all teams. I'm only betting two hundred dollars a game. Shit the first tomorrow, and I need to grab some extra work tonight." Don said.

I was cool with the bet, but often I liked to go higher. If it was two on two that little hundred dollars wouldn't do nothing for my pockets. So instead of taking their money, I would invest it into them when the bets were low. If they were higher, I would give them half. I gave the money to a different person each time so that I had a hand in all their pots. That's how I got my spending money so that most if not all of my checks went into the bank.

We played a few rounds, and the game even almost got physical at some points; however, just like any other time, my team took home the win.

"Y'all be cheating. Don and Dre can't be on teams no more. They played school ball and streetball together. I bet if you separate they asses, they would be corny." Joc complained.

"I ain't ever lost a ball game in my life so put me with whoever and the money still gone be mine. Anyway, while we were out here, I made need y'all to go check something out for me." I said seriously.

"What's up cuz you know I'll drop something for you," Don said, ready for war.

I ran down the situation with Kamirra down to them and told them to pay her and her brother a visit in a few days.

"Just check their temperature that's all, and force the issue of her changing her address and getting me a picture of it. Even if you got to take her down there. I don't want nobody getting hurt though unless it's absolutely necessary." I stood up from my seat.

"Man, give me back the old Dre. The one who used to toot guns and smoke weed all day. This nigga in the suit ain't working for me. You talking 'bout just check they temperatures. We already know they feeling some type which is why you should say go smack them up. I remember that time Rico tried to run up in the trap house. Mannn, Dre emptied a whole fucking clip without a word. He just got to busting. I'm in the back fucking a bitch and bullets start flying through the wall. I'm in that bitch rolling around butt ass naked trying to find my gun. Bout time I hit the hall I see a nigga running out the door. Dre still clapping at his ass, homie drove himself to the hospital and checked out right in front of that bitch." Don laughed.

"Listen, it was all fun when I ain't have shit. I trapped because I needed money and then I had a baby on the way. I always told you I didn't plan to stay in that shit. This life I have now is perfect for me. I will get my hands dirty if I have to, but it ain't like that no more. I don't really have any problems besides these two dumb ass broads, and that's just a consequence of dope dick. But aye hit my line if you need something and tell me when the next day y'all want to come to the courts I'm bout to go." I tossed the money to Juice Don's other boy.

He was quiet most of the time, and that was one of the reasons I fucked with him. He hustled, and he did it to get out, not so he could become the king of the streets. He was flashy but not too flashy, and he also worked at Popeyes to cover his tracks. I saw something in him, which was why the last few times the money went to him. Within two weeks, he had brought me at least five thousand.

I climbed in my car and saw that I had a missed call from Leah, dialing her back. I waited for her to answer.

"Hello." Her soft voice rang through the phone.

"What's good with you? I'm on my way home and figured I could order some dinner, and maybe you would want to come over, and we can have a redo." I said.

"I'm at the market, grabbing something for me to eat. I can cook it at your house if you want and we can eat that. Saves some money if that's cool with you." She replied.

"Bet, I eat just about anything, so surprise me," I said, then hung up.

Once I was home I made sure my house was cleaned and sat out a bottle of wine, I knew that she likes mimosas, so I got out the things for that as well and placed it on ice before going to take a shower.

Just as I finished my shower, I heard the doorbell ringing as well as my phone. I grabbed the phone and wrapped my towel around my waist. Ignoring Kamirra, I went walked out of my room.

"Who is it?" I called while jogging down the steps.

"Me," Leah answered.

I opened the door, and her eyes scanned over my dripping wet body. She slowly licked her lips once she eyed my print through the towel.

"Ole freaky ass, come in so I can put some clothes on or I can stay like this." ," I smirked.

"No, go put some clothes on while I start dinner. I hope you like pepper steak cause that's what I had a taste for. I grabbed extra and some containers so I can take some for lunch tomorrow to work and you can too if you like it." She smiled at me.

If her ass could cook, I was going to make her mines. I ain't care that we both just left a situation and I barely knew her. Shit, I would get to know her and keep her as mines just so she wouldn't get to know anybody else. Just the way she thought about me having lunch showed she was a caring woman. It may not have meant much to most people, but nobody ever made me lunch, so it meant a lot to me.

"I like that shit over rice with gravy. My mom be making that shit she ain't made it in a while for me. I'll be right back and make yourself at home." I told her before going to put clothes on.

I took my time getting dressed just so that I could allow her to get comfortable without me. I also was testing her to see if she would do anything else since I purposely left money on the counter. I wanted to see if she would return it or take it. I was hoping that she didn't take it. It put my mind at ease a little since she returned my wallet. However, there was no cash in there, so that did no justice for me. I came back down dressed in some sweats and a tank. She was at the stove playing music from her phone, and the money was still in the same spot. My stomach growled from the aroma of the peppers and onions she was mixing around in the pan.

"You must be hungry." She turned and looked at me.

"Very, you ain't go home and take off your work clothes first?" I asked.

"No, I went straight to the market after work. You mind if I add shrimp to yours or no?" She questioned while placing the steak in the sizzling pan.

"Do your thing beautiful, just make that shit with love," I said.

She smiled and turned back around. She moved around the kitchen like it was hers and I loved it. I opened up my laptop and checked out a few peoples backgrounds to kill time.

"Come try this gravy for me, see if I need to add anything." She called me over.

I stood up and walked over to her. She blew the gravy that was on the spoon before placing it to my mouth.

"God, please don't let her kill me cause this shit smells good." I prayed in my head, then placed the spoon in my mouth.

"Is it too early to ask you to marry me? That shit slamming, I was gone ask for a little bit cause I ain't know if you could cook, but let me taste that steak too since I'm over here." I told her opening my mouth for some.

She let out a small giggle but got the steak for me, again she blew it before placing it to my mouth. She surprised me again with them bold ass flavors. God was on my side cause this girl had a hand in the kitchen. I closed my eyes to savor the taste before I opened them only to see her staring at me.

"Well, did you like it?" She questioned.

"Hell yeah, I loved it," I told her, pulling her to me.

The intense stare down we were having was crazy. My eyes went from hers to her lips, and in that moment I wanted to kiss her. Hell, it felt like that's what was supposed to happen. So I inched closer to her face, she licked her lips like she was getting ready, but then that good ass gravy had to spill out of the pot causing us to pull apart. She quickly turned it off and cleaned up the mess that was made.

The rest of the night we spent eating and laughing until she was ready to go home for work.

"Thanks for dinner and my lunch, you gotta be my new best friend that cooks for me just until you ready to be my girl," I told her once she was in her car.

"That's cool, we can be best friends, make sure you lock up. I'll call you when I get home. Good night best friend." She laughed before pulling off.

"God if you just let me get that girl I promise I'll do right," I said out loud before going into the house.

I could get used to nights like this with her. The only thing that would have to change would be her leaving me. Instead of her going home, she would be climbing those steps for bed.

❧ 15 ❧

LEAH

"**B**oy, stop playing." I pushed Dre back.

He was in my face trying to kiss me for the third time today. Instead of having dinner together like we had been doing for the past week, I decided to bring him lunch since it was my day off.

"Nah, come here. Best friends are kissing now and shit on the low. You really came through for me. I was so used to having you make me lunch I ain't even peep until this morning you ain't have my shit in the fridge." He said before stuffing some Alfredo in his mouth.

"It ain't even been that long for you to get used to it. I'm bout to go, I have to go down to the bank. Hopefully, I got enough for this damn apartment." I sighed.

"That's why I don't get why you don't let me help you. We are best friends now, so you can't say no." He offered his help again.

I sat on top of his desk and looked at him. This man was gorgeous and so sweet. However, I knew that he had a mean side to him and I didn't want to be on the receiving end of that.

"I keep telling you, that whatever I get this time is going to get done by me so nobody can take it from me. My kids having a stable home has to be something no one can get mad and snatch back. I don't want to go through that again." I looked up at the ceiling to keep my tears from falling.

My kids were now a sensitive spot for me, and it had been almost two months since I had last them outside of an hour long visit once a week and those moments felt like they flew by. I feel like an hour wasn't enough time and I couldn't wait until I had more time with them.

"Shit gone get easier and I wouldn't take anything from you. I understand where you're coming from but you won't let me help you at all. Every angle I come from you shut me down. I just want to make them tears go away and see you smile." He wiped my eyes with his thumb.

"I know you are trying to help me and I appreciate it but I have to do this on my own. You don't understand this is personal for me, Quanny." I moved his hands from my face.

"I have to go." I told him while getting up.

I made it to the door before his strong arms were wrapping around me and pulling me back to him. I tried to hold in my tears but as soon as my back touched his chest I began to cry.

"Shh, it's alright. Damn, I'm sorry." He whispered in my ear.

"This is not fair, it isn't fair to me. I've been so depressed because I miss my kids. He has them up in a house with a bitch who just got her kids back. Why I just can't I be happy, I don't bother nobody. I can't even go around my cousins cause them bitches throw it in my face like it's okay. He tried to force me to get an abortion with my baby last year only to pop up with one by a bitch that was supposed to be his best friend's baby mom. I lost my child, and he wasn't even there for me, and now he's daddy of the year." I cried into his chest.

"Let it out," Dre told me. He pulled me down on his lap and listened to me. For the first time I opened up about my child and took me to a place I tried so hard to forget. My mind traveled back to the day I saw my baby for the last time.

Stepping out of my car in front of the funeral home on 42nd Street. I closed my eyes, and took a deep breath. It was a cold day but I felt hot inside, where I should have been shivering I was sweating. I had called Nymir and texted him so many times only for it to go unanswered. I was here by myself and I shouldn't be.

"Yo cous, you ready?" My cousin walked up on me.

"Where you come from?" I asked him while looking across the street at the funeral home.

"You told me you might need me so I pulled up on you. Come on man, you gone be late and it's pouring down out here. I got you." Kenny said.

Now Kenny wasn't my real cousin, he lived on the same strip as me when we were younger and his father's first cousin was married to my uncle on my dad's side. We hadn't found that out until after we had already started calling each other cousin.

"You right let's go." ," I spoke lowly.

We walked across the street and the closer we got to the building, the more my tears fell with the rain. The aroma of death hit me and I felt like I couldn't do it. I went to turn around, but Kenny pushed me forward.

"Come on cuz, you got to do this." He gave me a little push so I could step inside.

Turning around I went in and took a seat in one of the chairs that were in the waiting area. It was quiet inside and only gave you time to think. My stomach turned as the death smell grew.

"Hello, Ms Aleah, we're ready for you if you are." The funeral director I had met with three times had come out of a room.

"Okay." I said, slowly standing up.

I followed him to a room, and as soon as I hit the door, a slow church beat began to play. I stepped into the room and walked in between the rows of seats. At the end, my baby laid wrapped up in a blue blanket. His skin was still soft to touch; however, he was cold and hard. I couldn't find myself to pick him up, so I ran my fingers across his face. As I touched him my knees began to feel weak. I placed a kiss on his forehead and whispered I loved you and see you later just as the walls began to feel like they were closing in on me.

"God, why, please. I'm sorry, what did I do? Please give me my baby

back." I screamed as I felt myself falling to the floor. My cousin ran over and held me up.

A person came and wrapped my baby back up and took him through a back door where the freezers probably were. My legs felt like noodles as I forced my way back to the chairs out front.

"We will call you when his remains are ready, the urn you picked came in today. The last thing we needed to in the process before the cremation was to allow you to see him." The man said, showing no emotion.

"Thank you." I said I looked back at the room I had come from and whispered another I love you.

"Cous, calm down. I need you to focus, if you can't drive home I can take you but you have to let me know." Kenny held me by my shoulders.

The rains had slowed down and the sun was peeking through the thick clouds. I took that as a sign my baby had heard my final goodbyes. He knew while there were dark clouds I needed a little sunshine in my life.

"I'm okay. I'm good, I can make it home. I'm just going to sit here for a few seconds." I pulled away and went to walk across the street.

I stopped to let the bus go by when really I wanted to walk in front of it. My heart had a whole in it that only my child could fill. Crossing the street I got into my car and sat there. My phone went off and a message from an unknown number popped up. I opened it only to see Nymir sleep on a female's lap. Her small pudge was on full display, while her hand rested on his head. The text read "stop calling he's sleeping."

Instead of responding I put my car into drive and headed to my sisters house. She was my comfort through it all. Since she was at work I crawled in her bed and hugged a pillow. To help ease my pain I grabbed two of her Tylenol's off the table and took them to help me sleep.

"Damn, I'm sorry you had to go through some shit like that. And if you want me to be honest you should have let that man then. Wasn't nothing in the world was more important than that moment. All the things you allowed him to do to you while you were forgiving him was teaching him how to treat you." Dre commented.

"I know that, and I feel stupid everyday for allowing him to hurt me. I honestly wanted to hold on for my kids sake while at the same time being afraid to lose everything. I didn't want to be at where I am now. I wasn't happy but shit was stable. Plus I loved him, he loved me when I felt like no one else did." I went on.

"Don't make excuses for that man, he knew what he had and he knew what he could do. You don't deserve that. All you can do is learn from your mistakes and do better. Now you know what to take and what not to take in your next relationship. Whatever you feeling it's okay to feel just don't hold on to that feeling. Feel it and let it pass so you can get on to making those life decisions that best." Dre kissed my forehead.

"Thank you." I hugged him.

"Don't thank me. I'm always gone be here for you to talk to. Cause you've been there for me to talk to. Even if you hold out on me just remain my best friend for life cause I'm always gone be yours." He made known.

"You so sweet Quanny." I beamed.

Here it was I was just crying and this man had me smiling from ear to ear. He was making it very hard for me not to want to be around him all the time.

"Go meet with whoever you need to meet with. I have a meeting in an hour. After that we can link back up and look at apartments or houses. I just want to look with you, that's all. Plus I want to grab some properties, you could help me with that right?" He asked.

"Yeah, that's cool. I'll see you later, Bestie." I pulled him into another hug.

He held on to me and kissed my cheek before letting me go. I walked out of his office, feeling like a weight was lifted off of me. It felt good to talk to somebody other than my judgmental ass sister. It also made me think about Kenny and if he was still in jail. I would reach out to him as well as my bald bald-headed ass sister. It was time I stop sulking in the bad things and live my life while getting it on track.

❧ 16 ❧
DRE

Walking into my house, there was a piece of paper on the floor along with the mail. Picking it all up and opening the paper first I smiled hard when I saw the picture of Kamirra's new drivers license with her mother's address on it. Pulling my phone out I snapped a picture of it and emailed it to my lawyer letting him know to get on that soon.

My hardest most challenging days seemed to be the ones without my daughter, even though Leah was keeping me company there was nothing like having my child.

"Yeahhhh." ," I yelled out loud to no one in particular.

My day had just gotten ten times better than it already was. Now all I had to do was wait until the judge told that hoe to let me see my daughter. The thought of calling her and seeing if I could make it happen myself crossed my mind however doing it the right way was better.

Pulling my phone out, I dialed Kamirra's number, and she picked up on the first ring.

"I guess you got the paper." She said.

"Yeah, thank you for that. I hope you are doing better." I told her, and I really did, I just knew we were done.

"I'm cool, I would be much better if I was back home."

"That ain't gone happen we done for good this time. I can't be with you like that, and I'm not even sure if I could even be your friend. I need you to stop blowing my phone up." I sighed.

"I can't, and I won't. I love you, even though I don't act like it or show it. I'm ready to bare your children now whatever you want." She sniffed.

Instead of responding I hung up the phone. I wouldn't keep explaining myself to her for nothing.

"My baby finally get to come back with me." I shouted and danced around the house.

Dream had been asking for a new room so I figured I could go shopping and surprise her with a brand new room and clothes by the time she came back. Checking my phone I went through the room idea she had sent me from google before calling Leah to see if she could fix it with me.

"Yeah, I would love too. You have to wait until I get off though or start getting the stuff and we can do it when I get off. Hopefully I get this apartment I applied for last week. They said my background and stuff checked out but they ain't called me back yet. I'm so nervous." She spoke calmly into the phone.

"You gone get it, get back to work I know your ass in the break room that's the only time you answer my calls. Stop drinking all their coffee and check some people in." Before she could respond I hung up the phone.

My baby was really about to start coming over again, I couldn't wait for Leah kids to start coming back with her so that we could do play dates or whatever on the weekends. That way, I could still spend time with her, as well as having my little Dreamy.

A couple minutes later, my phone was ringing, and it was Shay.

"I need some money." She spat before I could say hello.

"For what?" I questioned knowing damn well I just sent a thousand dollar child support check.

"What do you mean? I have Dream don't I and I have a shut-off notice for the lights since somebody stopped paying all my bills." She sighed.

"I pay your mortgage, you can take care of the rest. You just received some money from me, you should have used some of that to pay your bills. I can't help you cause I ain't got it." I lied.

I had the money to help her, but I wasn't going to. It was no point in helping her when she never tried to help me. Shay yelled into the phone a bunch of cuss words and how I wasn't shit and would never see my daughter again. Usually, that would have me sending her the money she needed. This time I hung up the phone and waited for my lawyer's call.

Jackson never called me, but he did email me saying he would get everything to the judge, and I should be getting Dream soon.

I made my way into the kitchen to find something to eat. I usually had little things, but since my bestie had become a frequent visitor who liked to cook, so I had a bunch of options. Settling on a small salad that was in a bag. I poured some on a plate with ranch dressing and ate it.

My thoughts drifted off to Aleah, and I realize she may have been the girl for me. She just had to be, all we ever did was kiss and sleep in the bed together, and I already felt like I could possibly live with her one day. I wanted her to meet Dream as well as meet her kids. Hell, I could see us buying a big ass house and raising our kids together.

Banging on my door brought me from my thoughts, and I stood up. On my way to the door, I used my hand to touch the side of the table that sat by my door. A small drawer opened, and I grabbed my gun, cocking it and I asked who it was.

"Don." My cousin yelled back.

I swung the door opened, Don walked in as I decocked my gun and placed it back into its rightful place.

"What's good? How do you get this done for me?" I questioned showing him the paper.

"I just paid the bitch a visit she knew what I was coming for and her brother was on some he ain't want no work shit. I' am gone have some of my youngins keep an eye on him just in case. Plus the niggas he work with come to me when they got beef, so it ain't like he really got back up. They already know your blood. I came here on some shit though you know I'm getting money, but I'm finally trying to clean this shit up. I don't know what to do, and you know I can't get no nine to five my brain doesn't function long enough, and I'd be done got fired." Don explained.

"Man, stop letting people tell you that shit. All your life they told you that and you believed it. You can get a job you don't want to. I saw you focus long enough to sit and bag some weed and then crack right after. That shit takes a long time and if your ass can sit for hours to do that you can perform a job. You don't like to follow orders and want to be your own boss. I can respect that, shit, I know how that is. But don't sit here and tell me you can't focus long enough, my moms, your mom and everybody else all played a part in enabling you and as your big cousin I ain't gone allow that shit. You wanna make your money legally, you gone either get a job or get you a business, that's your best bet. Now when you find out what kind of business you want to run cause I know your ass ain't gone get no job you come talk to me bout that and whatever you need you know I got you." I promised.

He knew I meant it, Don was more like a brother to me. As we got older, we put more distance in between us. However, just like he would put his life on the line for me, I would do the same for him.

"I hear you big dawg. And man that's what everybody told me even the doctors so shit what I'm 'pose to believe. Aunty told me this broad named Leah got you walking around cheesing and shit. I know this ain't the jawn Amelia's sister. Cause if so man, you got you a bad ass broad. I been trying to fuck Amelia's hoe ass for years. That bitch like niggas with boku bread. She always talking about my money ain't long enough, but that's just cause I ain't never had to pay for pussy, so she was mad when I offered her forty dollars." Don said with a sigh of irritation.

"That's her sister and Amelia a hoe like that? Her sister ain't shit like her and I'm glad. Wait, you think my baby coulda been a hoe in the past? I mean she couldn't have been unless ole dude turned a hoe into a housewife, and hell if he didn't I'm willing to, and I dare a muthafucka to call my baby a hoe." I put out.

Shit I was lying to myself. just because she never showed hoe traits didn't mean she didn't have a little hoe in her. I was contemplating on telling Don to get word on her. At the same time I didn't want to ruin what we had. She never showed me that side of her. My mind was all over the place, and now I was frustrated.

My baby could probably be a hoe, and it was fucked up because I was feeling like I was falling for her, and I wasn't sure if I would be able to accept that. I had a daughter and I didn't want anyone telling her, her step mama was a hoe. Hell her mom was already a little on the wild side. I wanted to be with somebody she could talk to and confide in. And whenever she got old enough to deal with little boys and couldn't come to me, I wanted her to be who she turned to if not her moms. I couldn't do that if she was a young hoe cause that meant she would tell my baby to bust it wide open then I would have to kill her.

"Dawg, Leah, ain't no hoe. She always was with Nymir nut ass." Don answered my thoughts.

"A nigga was losing his mind over here." I laughed.

I silently thanked God because If Leah was a hoe, then I would have cut all that kissing and sleeping together shit out. She would still be my best friend, but I would friend zone her for real. Now I could continue to pursue my bestie in peace.

❧ 17 ❧

LEAH

Sitting at the desk of the rent office, I was shaking as I signed the last paper. The lady handed me my keys, and I jumped up and down. I ran out of the office and straight into Amelia's arms.

"Sis, I'm so fucking proud of you. You don't even understand. You did that shit baby, I told you, you could do it." Amelia held me in her arms.

All the long hours at work and saving finally paid off. I was able to pay my rent up for three months as well as my first, last, and security deposit. I shed a few tears before wiping my face.

"Only thing left to do is go shopping. Bitch I'll sleep on the floor before I go back to mommy house with all these people. Plus, Quanny finally got that shit he needed for his daughter to be allowed back so I know I can't be over there all the time no more until he introduces us." I said while walking to the car.

"I need to meet this man, he came in and swooped you off your feet. His must have got some good dick to have you making dinner, lunch, and all the other shit."

"I haven't even slept with him yet. I want to, but I just don't wanna fuck up what we got. I don't question him or anything right now, and you know once I get some I'm gone feel like he's all mine and that's not how it works." I replied.

"Bitch if you don't get some of that dick and stop playing. He gone fuck somebody else if you take too long. I'm telling you, niggas can only wait for so long. So get up on there and ride that nigga until he crazy about you." She said, rocking her hips like she was riding somebody.

"Girl shut the fuck up." I playfully pushed her.

The drive to my new apartment wasn't long, and I couldn't wait to just stick my key in the door. Before the car could fully stop, I was opening the door and jumping out.

"Slow the hell down," Amelia called from behind me.

I jogged up to the door and opened it. The first thing I did was take my shoes off since it had carpet which I didn't want, but hey it was a steal. I got a three-bedroom one-bathroom apartment for seven-fifty. It came fully equipped with a washer and dryer and all new appliances.

"This shit is nice. I like this open floor layout. Girl if you was really bout it you would call Mr. Quanny over and let him bust that pussy open all over this empty house. Shit, we have to clean the whole house anyway." She shrugged.

My mom always taught us that before we moved our furniture into a house we should do a thorough cleaning. And we followed her orders.

"Mommy gone be so excited I'm gone have to call her over so she could pick out my furniture." I replied while sitting on the counter.

"She is already on her way." Amelia said.

Nodding my head I looked around in amazement. I had to hold back my tears because I didn't want to cry any more. This was going to be the start of a new part of my life. My next house would be one that I brought. I didn't want to rent for long so instead of using my taxes to do a vacation like I usually did with the kids and my sister I would save it until I had enough to purchase a home.

"Get out your thoughts. Don't be over there, thinking of what you need to do next. Enjoy this first step, you accomplished something, stop acting like you didn't love. And why the fuck you ain't tell me you came across Shermaine's ugly ass again. Next time I see the bitch I'm trashing her. She need to learn how to mind her fucking business and worry about all them kids and which one of them dirty ass baby daddy's gone take her out the projects. And I'm gone tell your mother to keep our business far away from Auntie Sharlene. That bitch go run everything back to big Bertha." Amelia voiced.

"Ain't nobody worried about her, she can't beat me, and that's already been established. And your mom went to talk to her sister. We can't stop that, that's like somebody telling us don't tell each other everything. It's not Auntie's fault her daughter a hater." I responded.

"I guess we need to go food shopping here too. Did you pick the kids rooms yet?" She asked.

"Since the biggest room is that way I'm gone pick that and then the rooms over there I'll do the back room Callie's and the front Cion's. I was thinking of a Fortnite theme for C, and rolls for Callie." I expressed.

"That would be cute. That little girl loves her some Trolls. I' am going to buy Cion a PlayStation so he has a game over here and that's something you don't have to worry about."

"Thanks, sis." I smiled just as the doorbell rang.

Amelia walked over and allowed my mother into the house. I could hear her squeals from the door. I kept my spot on the counter and waited for her to step into the kitchen.

"Oh, I'm going to have fun with this. Hey, baby. Congrats on this place, it's beautiful. I'm so proud of you. It took you some time, but you ain't give up. Have you brought any cleaning supplies yet because I have some in my trunk y'all can go out and get. This place needs a cleaning. I need to move out that damn house I'm in, I know that's y'all nana's house, and y'all grew up in it, but I'm ready to sell it and move on. All y'all damn cousins come there like it's a shelter when they fall on hard times, and I can't do it no more." My mom got out.

She knew that even if she did move, she would still allow them to come and live with her.

"Lady please if you moved you would take them with you. I really think you should just get the house remodeled. It's not like you can't afford too. You haven't spent an ounce of nana's insurance money." Amelia said.

"She's right mom, use some of that and fix it. You shouldn't feel guilty about spending that. She left it for you and for you to take care of yourself and kids we grown now, and your house is the go-to for all of us. Even though I may not have slept there every night, you allowed me back in your home. Do something for yourself you know you would love to. Fix up that big behind basement and throw all our old stuff out and your siblings too or have them come get it. Whatever they don't want; put it in the trash. You can make a room down there and places couches down there and a bathroom and leave whoever needs to stay with you down there. That way your upstairs doesn't get messed up."

Sometimes my mom didn't like to hear what we had to say, but by the look on her face, I could tell she was thinking about it.

"Y'all may be right, Then I can get some new furniture as well. That's definitely something I'm gone do. Let's talk about this house and this man you have been entertaining. Amelia baby grab that damn stuff out the trunk." My mom said in one breath.

"Quanny, just my best friend, so why do we need to talk about him," I asked.

I tried to hold in my smile, but it was killing me to do so. I felt my cheeks betraying me as a smile spread across my face.

"That's why. He gots to be ugly if you hiding him and made the damn boy your best friend. However, he got to have some good ding a ling if you always sleep at his house." She said, looking at me.

"Same shit I said ma," Amelia said as she came in with a bin filled with cleaning stuff.

"Watch your mouth."

"Ma, he ain't ugly. Quanny is handsome. I'm talking fine as crap. We are best friends because we can confide in each other and we both just came from bad situations. I don't want that to cloud our judgement. Now, this is the last time I'm explaining this, oh and we ain't do the do yet." I said for the last time.

"Okay well, you wouldn't mind this then." My mom said, confusing me until I saw her pick up my phone and began talking.

"Yeah baby, come on over. Yes, that's the address, I can't wait to meet you either. See you soon." She smiled.

"Now Joy, I know good, and well you ain't answer my phone and tell him to come over here," I said, calling her by her first name.

"I sure and the hell did, I would like to meet this man, and it's clear as day you ain't about to do it no time soon, It was a sign from God, that man got to calling while we were talking about him. Won't he do it." She smiled.

Sucking my teeth, I grabbed the cleaning supplies and began cleaning. I wasn't ready for Dre to be meeting my mom or my wild ass sister. In fact, I didn't even know if we would ever reach the point in doing that and I didn't want to rush into things.

I knew he was just my best friend, so it shouldn't have been a problem, but at times I felt like we were so much more.

"She mad as hell so he got to be ugly Mi." My mom tried to whisper.

Ignoring her comment, I would let her see for herself. Not too long after the front door came open and Quanny walked in. I kept my head down like I didn't see him and continued to clean. He walked over to me and pulled me into a hug, making me smile.

"Congrats on the place, big head." He whispered in my ear.

"Thank you," I responded lowly.

I looked up at him and stared into his eyes, he leaned down to kiss me and before our lips could touch someone cleared their throat.

"Well hello, best friend," Amelia smirked.

"God damn." My mom said while grabbing her chest.

"What's good, and how are you doing ma'am," Dre spoke to my mother and sister.

Amelia dapped him up like she was one of the guys while my mom stood there like she was in shock. Dre walked over to her and pulled her into a hug.

"Good lord, I see why she was hiding this man. His momma had to be sleeping with a man of God to be blessed with this boy." My mom called out, causing us all to laugh.

"Thank you, you're beautiful yourself," Dre responded.

He turned to me and shot me a wink with a big smile, he was soaking that shit in. My mom fixed her hair and looked My Quanny up and down.

"Ma, you better stop. Leah is looking at you like she wants to curse you out." Amelia laughed.

"That shit not funny, he is way too young for her. That's all me right there." I admitted.

"Oh, I'm all you?" He asked, walking back over to me.

"You know what's up, you're my best friend, so that means you stuck with me for the long run." I tried to clear up my statement.

"I hear you. When you gone get some furniture?" He questioned.

I looked at him with a small frown. I knew where he was going with that statement. however, I would work to get the furniture. I had some money for it, but for the most part, I would get things room by room.

"Just know you can always ask and I'll make sure it gets done.

I can have the whole place furnished in one day." He threw his hands up in surrender.

"No, I already told you about that shi." I got out before he shut me up with a deep passionate kiss like my mother wasn't right there.

"That's the one for her." My mom said, saying something that I had been thinking lately.

18

DRE

My front door was wide open as I waited for Shay to bring my daughter to me. I had been sitting on the steps for about an hour and I was starting to feel like she wasn't coming. So I got up and came to get me a drink so I could wait a little longer.

"Daddy." I heard making me spin around and damn near run to the door.

I could hear her beads before I saw her. Once she was in my eye sight I dropped to my knees and held her to me. As much of a man as I was I couldn't stop the tears from falling down my face.

"That's a damn shame. Oh and I brought my boyfriend with me. This is Kirk, Kirk, that's my baby father, DreQuan." Shay introduced us.

I looked up and locked eyes with the man that shot at me when I was younger. Kirk was around forty years old and still a regular ounce selling hustler. He smirked and looked around my house.

"Oh, I see you finally made big dawg moves." He chuckled.

Bending down, I whispered in my daughter's ear, telling her to go to her room. I had been waiting for years to see this man. I promised him the next time I saw him he wouldn't leave breathing and I meant that.

"Y'all know each other ?" Shay asked, confused.

"Yeah real big pussy, You know I've been trying to see you for a minute right. You know it's been sometimes since you pulled that shit and fucked up thing is Shay I would have thought you remember the nigga who shot at us when we was on your momma porch. I'm sure he knows who the fuck you are. See you almost shot her while she was holding my baby and for that, I owe you." I replied.

Kirk went to reach in his pants I guess to grab his gun and I swung on him. My jab connected to his jaw making him stumble back. Now just because Kirk was old didn't mean he wasn't in shape. And I found that out when he threw a punch back that caught me in the jaw.

Laughing I faked with another right and when he jumped I caught him with a left dazing him. I slammed him against the wall and repeatedly punched him in the face. Kirk leaned over and pulled his gun out for a second we wrestled over it and a shot rang out. At that point Shay began to scream for us to stop.

Holding on to his arm I began stepping back, I checked to see if I was hit and where the bullet landed. I was happy when I saw it hit the back door.

Keeping my hold on his arm, I slammed my fist into his face. Saying fuck it I began to bang his arm on the wall until he dropped the gun. I grabbed him by his neck and kept him in a hold until he passed out.

"Alright, Dre he out. Let him go before you kill him." Shay tapped me.

"That's the fucking point, you think he gone live to come back to my house?" I yelled at her.

I knew soon the cops would come, I lived in a good neighborhood and gunshots weren't normal in these parts.

She looked at me and must have realized I had snapped back in my old ways. I remember when we were younger, she used to look at me that same way when I would be about to get into it with a nigga. Sighing, she walked towards the steps.

"I really liked this one, but do what you have to do. Be safe DreQuan I'm going to sit here and make sure Dream doesn't come down just until crazy comes." She said while sitting at the bottom of the steps.

I nodded and grabbed my unregistered gun. Screwing the silencer on it, I dragged him to my backyard.I pressed play on the surround system and turned the music up. I quickly called Don and told him to pull up on me for that card game we use to play.

I knew he got the memo when he said he would bring some people to play with us.

"God forgive me for my sins." I prayed.

I pointed my gun and shot him twice in the head, I was glad that you couldn't see into my backyard. I left him out there and went to answer the banging on the door, Shay stopped me and went herself. I backed up into the kitchen turning the music down and listened.

"Who is it?" She questioned.

"Police."

I heard her unlock the door before opening it.

"Good afternoon officers." She spoke politely.

"We were just responding to a call for shots fired. We are going to each house to see if they heard anything." One responded.

"I didn't hear anything as the music was playing loudly while I cleaned up. Could you please leave me a card and I'll give you guys a call." She faked concern.

One thing I loved about Shay was that she was into the streets and knew how to lie. I knew for a fact she wouldn't fold under pressure either. We had been through enough to know that no matter how much she said she hated me, she would never see me in jail if she could prevent it.

The cops gave her a card and went on their way. Shay closed

the door back, and moments later, Don came walking through the basement door.

"What's good?" He asked, pulling his gun from his waist while looking at Shay with murder in his eyes.

"Boy, not me I don't want shit to do with this. Dre just gone have to make up for the money he was giving me." She said with a frown.

"Man, I had to come through the side entrance it's hot as fish grease out there. I got my silencer on my gun, though, and the boys were pulling off as I was coming up." Don spoke.

"Backyard," I said.

Don nodded he went back out front, and got inside his truck, pulled it around. Once he got the nigga wrapped up in the plastic I gave him a few bands and the gun.

"Now I gotta get you another one." he laughed.

I dapped him up, and he was on his way. I knew he was gone, take the body and gun and probably cremate that shit together. Don acted like he didn't have connections, but he did. His grandpop on his dad's side owned a funeral home, and he often used that to get rid of shit.

"I'm about to go. DreQuan, please don't ever do no shit like that again while my daughter is upstairs. Now I got to find me another nigga dumb enough to give me all his money. And I wasn't playing. I'm gone need some hush money from you." She said.

"Don't even act like that, I got you. But you know damn well it ain't no hush money. Don't act like you so innocent, it's a couple niggas rotting cause you needed them to be. So let's not act like that." I reminded her.

When we first got together, her uncle and his friends gang-raped her. When she told me I was so mad and didn't think twice when I went and sat the whole house on fire with them in it. She had even made sure she came to help me. While I coated the back with gasoline, she coated the front. She even went inside and turned the stove on so the gas could escape. I made sure they were all high and stuck. I waited by the back door, and anyone who tried to run out would have got shot.

"Now, just bring up my past. Enjoy time with your daughter. I see you on Sunday." She said before walking out.

I locked the door and went upstairs with Dream. Her tablet was playing, but she was fast asleep. Instead of waking her up, I let her take her nap so that I could shower.

After I finished up my shower, I called Aleah so she could help me bake cookies while on face time. She directed me on the cookies and a cake until I was done.

"Thanks Leah," I said before hanging up.

A little while after Dream came down and we washed her hands and decorated the cake together.

"You want to help me with this?" I asked her, pointing to the stuff for pizza biscuits.

"Of course." She answered with a smile.

I picked her up and sat her on the counter as we made our food.

"I missed you, daddy." She told me.

"I missed you too, my favorite girl. What have you been up to? I see you lost another tooth." I replied.

"Nothing, mommy and I did a lot of shopping, and I had camp a lot." She said.

"How did you like camp? Anybody been bothering you? Did you make any friends? Are your teachers cool? Tell me about it." I asked questioned after question.

"I made a lot of friends, but one and I don't know why. This boy named Matthew always messes with me. Mom had to come up there, and she yelled at his mom, and he stopped. It's fun besides that stuff." She responded.

"Sometimes, people are just mean because maybe they are not happy or someone is being mean to them. People like that you ignore unless they put their hands on you or you just can't take it anymore. You should have told me, I would have come and knocked him out for you." I told her.

"It's all good. It was still great even with him not liking me. It just made me sad sometimes because he did it every day."

I nodded my head, and we finished making our food and got snacks. We climbed on the couch and watched Trolls world tour and Barbie movies. I looked over and smiled at Dream if I had to watch these kinds of movies forever to make her happy I would. I loved my daughter so much, and I was finally feeling whole again.

19

LEAH

G od had been so good to me this past week, my apartment was finally looking like a home, and the judge had just granted me partial custody of my babies. Both of their rooms were fixed up while I only had a bed in mine. I had been pulling extra shifts all week to make sure my check this week was double the size. It meant sacrificing time with Quanny, but I was glad he understood. I finally had some shit of my own and even though I didn't own it the only person that could get me put out was me.

"Thank you so much, so tomorrow I can get them, right? Nymir, is it okay if I pick them up from school? They have clothes and everything already. I'll be sure to have their uniforms back to you Sunday night with them?" I asked Nymir.

We were standing outside of the courtroom, and I was finally able to walk out of that room with a smile on my face. I wanted to bring up the divorce papers and making sure he would sign them, but I didn't want to mess anything up.

Since it was Thursday, I was able to get them from Friday to Sunday. I wanted to ask him if we could do it from Thursday until Sunday just so I could get them tonight, but I didn't want to push it too far right now. I would wait until we were on better terms.

"Yeah, that's cool. Their bedtime and everything is the same. I see you have been taking care of yourself." He smiled at me.

"Yeah, and thanks," I replied before walking off.

I still wasn't ready to have a conversation with him. Eventually, we would have to talk; however, I couldn't stand to look in his face. Not only did he show up to court like he was the best father in the world, he brought his bitch with him, and they both could kiss my ass.

From the courthouse, I went straight to walmart Walmart to grab drinks and snacks I knew the kids loved. Our first night back together was going to be a game night, and the next would be a movie night. I would plan something fun for them every weekend.

"Oh hey, back at my mother's house." My cousin Shermaine said from behind me.

She had a shopping cart full of shit letting me know her food-stamps had just hit. She had to know my business through our mother's daily conversations and gossiping.

"Hey, Ms. can't stay in my own business. You know, I keep telling you if you applied as much attention to finding a job or taking care of your kids you wouldn't be so focused on me. Oh, and if your ass went to the market to get meat instead of doing all your food shopping in Walmart, you wouldn't run out so fast. Now I'm having a good day and don't want you to ruin it so hurry up before your ride leaves you. God bless big cousin." I waved goodbye to her and continued my shopping.

After I double-checked things I needed off my list, I went to self check out and paid for my items. While placing my stuff in the trunk, I felt a pair of arms wrap around me, causing me to jump hard and drop my keys. A smile quickly formed on my face as I smelt his way too familiar scent.

"You so fucking scary," Dre whispered in my ear.

"If you know that why would you scare me. Got me dropping my stuff." I replied, stepping out of his embrace and picking up my keys.

"You know I like this natural look on you, but you gotta tame this shit at some point." He changed the subject.

"Boy, don't play with me. You like my ponytail." I frowned, rubbing my hands over my ponytail.

Maybe it was time for me to get back into the salons and start looking good. However, my sole focus had been on working and getting everything situated for my kids to return, making pampering myself the last thing on my mind.

"Before I forget how did court go?" He questioned while putting the last of my bags into the trunk.

"They're coming over tomorrow, I can't wait. I gotta stop by the market after I drop this home to go get meat and stuff like that. It feels so unreal, it also feels like tomorrow is taking so long to get here." I beamed.

"I'm happy for you, I ain't ever seen you cheese this hard it looks like your cheeks hurt." He laughed.

Dre closed my trunk and then pushed me against it, locking me between him and the car. He looked down at me and stared into my eyes. Licking his lips, he leaned down and pressed them against mine. His arms held on to me, pulling me closer as I slid my tongue into his mouth. We tongue wrestled for a few seconds when he squeezed my ass and pulled on my ponytail. I let out a soft moan.

"Shit." He groaned.

"Well I be damn, I know I taught you how to act in public. You stepped away from us for a few seconds only for us to find you lip-locking in Walmart parking lot." I heard which caused me to push him back.

"Daddy, you got a new girlfriend?" The little girl from the picture who I knew as Dreamy asked.

"Mom y'all causing a scene." Dre laughed.

"Scene you the one that was about to make a movie out here on a car." His mom yelled.

I buried my face in his chest from embarrassment while he laughed like it was funny.

"Oh god, at least let me say hi to the damn girl. Don't be shy now, miss lip lock." His mom kept on.

Dre stepped aside, and I looked at two female versions of him. I'm sure if my cheeks could turn red, they would have been.

"Hi, I'm Aleah, and Quanny is my best friend." I introduced myself.

"Best friend? Child, y'all and these titles. I'm Carmen, his mother, and this is Dream, his daughter. It was nice meeting you don't be a stranger. I need to get to know you." Carmen advised me.

"Hi, Ms Leah, you're pretty, but your ponytail is a little messed up friend." Dream pointed out.

"What I tell you about that mouth, you act like we ain't at least taught you manners you've been with your damn mama too long," Ms. Carmen said to Dream while pulling her towards the store.

Next time Dream saw me I was gone have my hair done so she wouldn't be able to talk about me again. Hell if a kid noticed then I must have been out there looking bad.

"She only said that cause I popped your hair tie when I pulled your hair. So now it's no longer in its ponytail." Dre laughed, making me smack his chest.

"Bye, I'm leaving," I told him while getting into my car.

He closed my door for me and walked off. Instead of pulling off, I sat in the car and dialed Nymir's number.

"Hello."

"Oh god, Nymir. I know we just saw each other in court earlier. However, the kids have been on my mind. I've been calling you for some time now and haven't gotten an answer. The only time we speak is at court, and I wanted to know if there was some way I could see or speak with the kids. It's been about six days since you let me talk to them and I really miss them. Please, I can't do this, I didn't want to bring it up in that building in fear of it being an argument." I began.

"Cause I found out about your new man six days ago. If you

really wanted to contact them why you ain't pulled up, you know where I live. You are not as good of a mother as you seem you let some dick distract you. My kids are good, and they don't need to talk to you, yeah you called, but that's it." He snapped and gone was the civilized parent he was in front of his girlfriend earlier this morning.

"I didn't come because I didn't want to mess up anything with court. I tried to abide by the rules. You know I miss them, nobody made me forget about them. Nymir, you know how I feel about them. Please just let me hear their voice then." I pleaded with him.

"I don't know shit, don't speak on that court shit like that's why you mad at me, not my kids. So don't take it out on them. How you think they feel, have you thought about that. I may have not picked up, but you know you could have pulled up. My locks ain't changed." He replied.

"I don't have a key to that house anymore, and I have thought about them, which was why I called and have been calling. You don't answer. I swear to God I just didn't want to cause anything that could hurt me in this case. I'm really trying my best to get everything on track so that they can be with me again. I just want them to know that. I know they miss me. I'm begging you, why do you want to hurt me so bad?" I began to cry.

"Here you go with that crying shit Aleah, you been crying for years now. When you gone stop, that shit is depressing. You are too old to be sitting around crying. If you want to talk to your kids, do what you have to do. I know I fucked up but you can at least forgive me, I forgave you for killing my baby, and I forgive you now for talking to that nigga like you not my wife still." He spat.

"I did not kill my child, I was stressed out because you couldn't find a job. On top of that, you were fucking everything with legs. Then you had the nerve to be trapping and couldn't help me with shit. But you found time to pop bottles at the club with your friends and whatever else you decided to do. While I paid the bills, took care of the kids, worked, and was carrying a baby. So if anybody needs to be sorry, it's your ass. Now I tried to be respectful and do things right. I'm tired of you feeling like you run shit. Not anymore Nymir, I'm gone get my fucking kids, and I'm going to talk to them." I screamed into the phone.

Nymir let out a soft chuckle before hanging up. If I still knew him right, he would be dropping them by his momma house tomorrow, and I would be stopping by. He didn't want to play fair, and I wasn't going to play by the rules no more either, hell the judge already granted me partial custody. Saying fuck waiting until tomorrow I pulled off driving straight to his house. It wasn't my intended destination, but since I was here, I hopped out of my car and banged on the door until someone opened it.

"Mommy," Callie called from behind Morgan.

She ran right into my arms, and I hugged her so tightly.

"Baby, I missed you sooo much." I held onto her while rubbing her back.

"Fuck is you doing here?" Nymir questioned.

"I'm seeing my kids like you said. I'm not trying to take them yet. But I deserve this, I'm there mom. Ciooonnnn baby," I called from the door.

Cion came running from the direction of the backyard. He almost knocked me over when he ran into me to pull me into a hug.

"Mommy, I've missed you so much. Daddy said that you haven't been calling. You don't want to talk to us no more?" Cion held my face.

"Big boy, you know I always want to see and talk to y'all. Mommy got us a new house so soon y'all can come over. I have been calling to tell you two, but I guess daddy's phone has been messing up or something. Gosh, you both are getting so big. Cion is that a tooth missing?" I was so excited to see them; I couldn't cry. All I could do was smile and hold on to them.

Nymir stood and watched us the entire time, while Morgan went back into the house. I didn't care about either of the two and what they did still hurt, but I couldn't change it, so why bother with it. After about twenty minutes of sitting on the ground with my babies, Nymir called them in for dinner. I hugged and kissed them, we said our I love yous and they went into the house. I could tell they didn't want to go in, but they followed their father's orders anyway.

"Thank you Nymir, that meant a lot to me. I know you said some foul shit earlier and I forgive you. I just want to be cool for the sake of our kids. You don't have to respond to that now but just think about it. This is only hurting them in the long run." I expressed before walking off and leaving.

My whole day was just made perfect, and in the situation we were in, I couldn't have asked for more at the time.

20

DRE

My mom's house was packed as usual on the Fourth of July. Everybody was outside, and being as though she now lived down the bottom people walked by to see the fireworks. Every year they threw a big block party and outside was full of people.

"Dre, what time is Ms. Leah coming and is she really going to bring her kids?" Dream asked excitedly.

Normally, I didn't allow her to play with kids, so it was always only just her. I had that knock a kid the fuck out mentality as a dad, especially for my daughter.

"Yeah, she said she would be here soon. Are you gone finish helping your glammy, finish up the strawberries? You doing a good job." I approved of her work.

The strawberries were beautiful in my eyes. My baby dipped them in white chocolate and made blue lines on them. Now the lines were a mess but if anybody told my baby that I would curse they asses out.

"Thanks, daddy." Dream sang.

I nodded my head then walked out of the kitchen, I checked my phone once more before going to lay down—the amount of drinking I planned on doing I needed to take a nap before it could happen. Closing my eyes, I fell into a deep sleep.

༺❀༻

"WAKE YOUR ASS UP." I HEARD, FEELING A WEIGHT ON TOP of me.

I automatically knew who it was by her voice. Holding on to her hips, I pressed into her before sitting up.

"Wassup baby, you brought the kids?" I questioned, looking around for them.

Instead of seeing kids, I saw the taller skinner version of my bestie.

"What's up, sis?" I spoke.

"Ain't shit bro, Don, your cousin? That nigga gets on my damn nerves. If I knew he was here, I wouldn't have come. I mean he would be alright if his breath didn't smell like he got a bad tooth." She frowned.

"Don't do my boy like that." I laughed.

She wasn't lying, but I would never tell her that nor would I let her play my cousin. I tapped Leah's thigh so she could get up.

"How did you get in here?" I asked her.

"Your mother let me in. She said you were on the couch, sleeping, so I came in here. And yes my kids are here. They are out front playing with Dream. We should go out there so everyone can formally meet." She said

"Cool," I said, standing up.

"I see some potential money out there, and it's still early." Amelia rubbed her hands together like she was a nigga.

I shook my head at her before running to the bathroom. After pissing and handling my hygiene stuff, I made my way back downstairs. Leah and Amelia were in the kitchen with my mom talking.

"Come on, then I have to come back and help your mom in

the kitchen. Amelia gone hold it done for now, though." Leah said, pulling me out of the kitchen.

We made our way outside and searched for the kids. After about two minutes, we found them bouncing around in the moon bounce while the DJ played old school music. The old heads were dancing around or on their grills. I couldn't wait to do stuff like this when I got old.

"Cion, Callie, and Dream. Come here." Leah called for the kids.

They all came out after a few seconds and were smiling.

"Okay, so Cion and Callie, this is Dre, or you guys can call him Quanny like I do. He's mommy's best friend and Dream is his daughter." She spoke calmly.

"Hi, can we go play now," Cion said, ready to go back to the moon bounce.

"No, I'll tell you when you can go back, now listen. While we are here, you have to follow Quanny's directions. If something goes wrong, he will protect you as well as he is an adult. Make sure you ask him if not me if you want something, or you can ask his mom. The nice lady who told you guys y'all could come out here and play or come in and get what you want. Be nice to Dream, and y'all look after each other." She replied sternly.

"Yes, mom." Callie and Cion said in union.

Then it was my turn I looked at Dream, and she smiled at me, causing me to smile back.

"Dream this is Aleah, Callie and Cion. Be nice, play, and have fun. If somebody messes with y'all come tell me, and I'm gone get that kid and their parents. Don't go anywhere without telling one of us, and most importantly, don't go with anyone you don't know. Other than that, have fun." I finished up my speech.

The kids nodded and ran off back to the moon bounces. They didn't really care what we were saying, and they didn't even try to act like it. I was happy that they were playing together and not fighting.

"They ain't give a damn about what we were saying. Let me

go help your mama. You think she gone to ask me about us? You notice people swear we are more than best friends?" She looked at me.

"Yeah, I noticed. I really don't give a fuck though. It's whatever between us, you know how I'm coming behind you. I ain't gone lie, if you ever tell me you ready, I'm gone snatch you up. I refuse to let you become somebody else's cause I feel like you already mine." I told her honestly.

"And that's probably why they think that cause you are saying shit like that and you will say it in front of anybody." She said.

"What I'm pose to lie?" I frowned at her pulling her to me.

"No, hell I don't know. Let me just go help your mom." She pulled away from me.

I watched as she went into the house and probably into the kitchen. I knew damn well my mom was gone, making her feel comfortable while getting her whole life story at the same time. She would then tell me what she felt about her once she left or any chance my mom got to talk to me alone.

Looking around, I spotted the kids in line for cotton candy, walking over to some of the boys I watched on as the played dice. My right hand was itching, and that let me know I needed to get in on the game.

"Yo, let me play," I spoke, making them all look up.

"What's up old head, let me holla at you after this," Juice told me.

"Cool, you straight?" I questioned.

He nodded his head, his ass shook the dice and threw them.

"Run me my bread." He told everybody with his hand out.

We all paid up, and I waited for my turn. Once I got on the dice, it was like I never was coming off them. I played for a while until Don pulled up and came and got me.

"This nigga always take everybody money his ass got fucking magic hands." One of the local drug dealers who name I wasn't sure of said.

"I played dice my whole life youngin ', and it never let me down. Aye, Juice whenever you are done, get at me." I said before walking off with Don.

"Kirk people pose to be looking for the person that had him come up missing. We can go at them full force or see if they ever catch up to us. You think your baby mom is gone let them know." He asked while we walked back to my moms to grab a drink.

"If they come they come, You already know how that's gonna end up. I ain't running from nobody. You know Shay is solid, even though she makes my life hell she always has been solid. That girl ain't never told, I honestly think she doesn't remember him. If it comes down to that though it's gone get handled." I shrugged.

"If that's ya word then I'm taking it. You already know I'll take the rap for you, you the one that made it out and gave the rest of us hope. Shit the only thing that's destined for the rest of us is jail or a graveyard. You chose a different route, and you gave us all some shit to talk about. So if it comes down to it let that shit fall on me, the family needs you more, you more valuable." Don started.

Anytime problems sparked up he got like that, he swore he owed me something because I helped him get started and then I gave him more to get ahead once I left the game and he did it on his own.

"Our family needs you too, and ain't shit gone happen. We got muthafuckas that will give their life for us, and that right there means we both are valuable. Just like you would lay down for me, I would for you. I'm a man first, and I appreciate you for saying that shit but what's done is done. If I gotta lose all this shit behind my respect then Ima risk it all. You feel me? Now if the problem comes, they come. That's more than likely that's them dirty ass young bulls he ran with trying to make a name not knowing he wasn't seeing no real bread." I responded.

Aleah came out of the house followed by Amelia, they sat on

the porch with cups in their hands laughing. I watched them just happy to see them happy. Hell Amelia was just as beautiful as Aleah. But my baby was something different. We locked eyes, and she shot me a wink which I returned. Her sister said something, causing her to cheese.

"You ain't tell me my future wife was here, let's go," Don said damn near skipping the rest of the way.

I walked up on the porch and took a seat next to Aleah. She placed her feet up on my lap, and I took in her look. She had on some blue denim shorts, with a 76ers shirt and some white sandals. Amelia had on the same fit except her shirt was a crop top.

"What are you drinking?" I took her cup and sipped it.

I could taste the Hennessy a little but overall, it was fruity.

"Amelia was in there making me and ya mama drinks. Your mom made her make a whole damn container talking bout that Henny punch for everybody. I see your family starting to come." She said, looking at Don, who was almost drooling over her sister.

"Yeah, Don this my bestie Leah, and you already know her sister." I introduced them.

They waved to each other before Aleah turned her attention back to me. She looked at me then got up and walked into the house. Aleah came back minutes later with the big bottle of Hennessy that wasn't opened and some cups.

"Thought you would want a drink and him too." She said, sitting back down.

We all sat on the porch laughing and talking. Amelia and Don smoked so much you would have thought the grill was on the porch with us.

The sun had finally gone down, and all my family was over. Every time someone new came, I had to introduce them to my bestie. Eventually, I didn't even care to introduce them and my mom had to do it for me. She had come out on the porch after Aleah had fed the kids and gave them money for water ice.

"Aleah, if you don't mind I'm going tell the kids to come play in the backyard. Dream has a swing set and all kinds of shit to play with. It's getting dark, and all the fun things for them to do are leaving." My mom said.

"Go head Ms Carmen, I was gone get them in a few but if you want you can thank you. Let me know if you need me to do anything." Aleah replied sweetly.

Her words came off a little slurred and I knew she was drunk hell I was too. We had almost finished the bottle and had shared more stories then I could count. I would never know her little ass was the bad one between the two growing up.

The kids had come back and ran into the house to go play out back. Callie stopped for a second and came over to us.

"Mom, this is so fun, can we come back here all the time?" She asked.

"Yes, if Ms Carmen lets you," Aleah answered.

Callie jumped up and down before running to the back yard. My mom didn't come back so I knew she probably stayed back there with them and the old folks. They probably were playing cards and talking shit to each other.

My phone dinged letting me know I had a message. Pulling it from my pocket, I read over it and almost choked off my drink.

Bestie - Walk me to the bathroom right quick, I wanna taste you since you look so good.

I had to look at her, then look back at the text. My dick instantly bricked up and as bad as I wanted to say no, I couldn't. While everybody else was talking and laughing, I grabbed her hand and pulled her up.

I led her upstairs to the bathroom. I knew nobody would come up because my mom made everybody go to the bathroom downstairs. She didn't play people coming up her steps.

Once I closed the door, Aleah was on her knees, pulling my pants and boxers down. She grabbed my tool and kissed it before running her tongue alongside it. I took in a deep breath and let my head rest against the door.

"Fuck." I groaned when she took me into her mouth.

She bobbed her head up and down while twisting her hands at the base of my dick. Aleah opened her mouth and stuck her tongue out. Every time she took me deep in her throat, her tongue would touch my balls. I grabbed her hair and pumped into her mouth.

"Mmm." She moaned, almost making me bust.

Pulling her up, I lifted her off her feet. Sitting her on the sink, I stepped out of my pants and bent down. Her pussy smelt so good. I pulled her shorts off of her and lifted her legs over my shoulders. I blew lightly before I let my lips lock on her pearl.

"Quanny." She moaned while I snacked on her.

I let my tongue twirl around her folds, and I even slipped it in her hole a few times. She began to scoot away, so I pulled her closer. Once she was at the edge of the sink, I licked my thumb and then slowly entered the tip of it in her ass while I sucked on her clit.

"Ahhh, shit." She screamed as her body shook. I kept on going until she was shaking like she was convulsing.

I stood to my feet and held her legs in the crook of my arms. She grabbed my face and kissed my lips. While we kissed, I rubbed the tip of my dick against her folds before slowly sliding into her. We both let out a gasp, and I thanked God for her. Aleah's pussy was so tight.

Pumping slowly in and out of her while sucking on her neck had her screaming, and I didn't even care to tell her to be quiet. I felt good knowing that I was making her feel like that.

"Shit, ooouuu, that's my spot." She called out.

"Yeah, well I'm bout to beat that shit up," I whispered into her ear.

Pulling her down, I made her bend over while placing one leg up on the counter. I had to bend a little to slide in her, but once I was in there, I showed her no mercy. She held on the counter and let her head fall down. I grabbed her by her hair and pulled her head up. Aleah's eyes were closed while she chewed on her bottom lip.

"Look at me, Aleah. Look at me while I fuck you." I growled.

She opened her eyes, and I felt like I fell in love as we stared at each other through the mirror. I placed my thumb back in her ass and pumped as hard as I could. My other hand was squeezing her plump ass while she cried out.

"I'm bout to cum, daddy ooouuu this shit feels so good." She yelled.

"Cum on your dick then, let that shit out baby." I hissed.

"Ohhh god." She called out as her body shook.

Her walls clamp down on me, and she let her head drop again as she came turning my dick white. I kept on pumping, and she began to squirt all over me. Aleah was screaming so loud I had to place my hand over her mouth. I fucked her until my balls got tight and my knees got weak, I began to let my nut out. What I was doing crossed my mind, and I quickly pulled out of her letting my seeds spill out on her back. Aleah quickly turned around and dropped to her knees and sucked the rest of it out of me. She kept on sucking even when I was empty.

"Hell nah, get off of me you the devil," I told her, pulling away from her.

She smirked at me before standing up. I handed her a washcloth while getting one for myself. Looking in the closet, I grabbed new toothbrushes and handed her one. We cleaned up ourselves, and the bathroom then returned to the party. For the rest of the night, I was smiling. She hadn't even known it, but that ass was mine, and I was sure I loved her.

❧ 21 ❧

LEAH

I woke up on the couch wrapped in Dre's arms. I looked around and saw Amelia sleep on the other couch and Don on the floor. Easing my way out of his arms without waking him. I stood up and tapped Amelia until she woke up. She rubbed her eyes and stretched.

"I'm going to find the kids, then we can go," I whispered.

She nodded and looked around before laying her head back down.

I was surprised to see the house was spotless and looked like a party never took place. I wasn't sure when we fell asleep, but I slept good. Finding the bathroom, I went inside and used it. While peeing, I realized that Dre had put a hurting on me. My shit was still sore from last night. After wiping myself and washing my hands I looked at myself in the mirror with disappointment.

I knew what I was doing and I let my horny ass do some shit without thinking twice. I really didn't want to confuse things between us when I hadn't even focused on divorce papers just yet. On top of that, I know his ass probably was looking at me like I was a hoe. I willingly sucked his dick in his mother's bathroom with a house full of people. I gave it right up while my kids were downstairs like I ain't have no cares in the world.

Walking out of the bathroom, I found my kids sleep inside of the guest room. It had toys in there so I was guessing this was Dream's room when she came over. I picked up Callie and then took her downstairs before coming back to get Cion.

Amelia picked up Callie and we headed towards the door. I opened it and was met by Ms Carmen.

"Hey girls, you leaving? I went out and brought all this stuff so we could do breakfast." She smiled.

I instantly felt guilty about trying to sneak out and turned back around. I walked back upstairs and placed the kids back in bed then came back down.

"Sis I know that sneak out if it was good don't feel bad about it," Amelia said as we made our way to the kitchen.

I looked at her and smirked. We walked into the kitchen and washed our hands.

"So, I hope you girls both enjoyed yourself. I also wanted to thank y'all for the help yesterday since my sister's ass came late." Ms Carmen thanked us.

"No problem." We both answered.

"How have you been this morning. You look tired you sure you don't want us to take over for you?" Amelia offered.

"No, it's fine, with you both helping we should be done in no time. Plus I still have to go out back and get my yard together. That's what I get for having all that damn punch you made." She laughed.

"It was good, wasn't it. And don't worry, we can help you with that too." I yawned.

I was still tired as hell, and my mouth felt dry. Seeing as though she still had cases of water, I grabbed one and downed it. We made small talk while we cooked. Once the food was done, I went upstairs and got all the kids up. With the okay of Ms. Carmen I went into the closet and grabbed new toothbrushes and rags. We all brushed our teeth together and cleaned our faces before heading downstairs.

Amelia had their plates made and ready at the table with cups of orange juice and chocolate milk.

Once the kids were eating we headed to the back yard. I cleaned while Amelia smoked.

"I can see it all over your face that you are feeling guilty about whatever. If you wanted to do it and did it, be happy with it as long as it was good. Don't regret the decisions you made because at the time you wanted them." She reassured me.

"I know I just can't help but feel like we took the next step when we ain't even really got a title. I mean yeah we are best friends, and we come to each other about everything, but I can't help but feel like it's so much more to us sometimes. I honestly felt like I loved that man when I looked up at him in that mirror. Then I feel like a hoe, his momma was down here watching my kids while her son was up there giving me the best dick of my life. We ain't even gone speak on how I'm still fucking married and haven't even taken any steps to get a divorce." I expressed

"Ain't nothing wrong with being a hoe. And you're not wrong for loving him if you do. You said it yourself you can go to him about anything and vice versa. Hell if I felt like that about a man I would have given him some as soon as my feelings changed. It probably would have been before that though to help me with my feelings. I can't love nobody or even be with them if the sex is weak. When it's time for that divorce to happen, it will. He knows you're married and ain't say nothing so cross that line when you get there. And even if this doesn't work if it makes you happy for the moment, enjoy it." Amelia preached.

I nodded my head and placed the last toy in the toy chest. I folded up the extra tables after wiping them down. Ms Carmen came out and frowned at me.

"I went upstairs to take a call and your little ass done came out here cleaned up. I told you I could do it. But thank you anyway." She said while coming out with a glass in her hand.

"What's that you're drinking?" Amelia asked.

"Mimosas. It's some in the kitchen." She said.

Amelia got up to go get her one and hopefully me too, cause I needed it. The door opened, and Quanny stepped out. He said good morning to his mom and kissed her cheek. He came over to me and pulled me into a hug whispering good morning and thank you into my ear.

"Let my future daughter and daughter-in-law go, we're out here having mimosas and girl time. Well, when Amelia comes back anyway. You bout to try and hog her so you can take her upstairs to my bathroom again." She said, making me smack his chest.

"I don't know what you're talking about." He smirked before letting me go and walking back into the house.

"I'm sorry" I got out just as she said don't worry about it.

"We all did that at some point in time, so I'm not worried about that. What I am worried about is you breaking my son's heart because you're scared. I'm also worried about you breaking your own and making the wrong decision. Let me tell you something if it feels right and different from anything else you've ever experienced, baby that maybe it. Now I see how y'all act and how y'all supposedly best friends, don't let crossing that line erase everything y'all built before that. Especially if it had you feeling like you loved him." She said, sipping her drink.

Nosey ass. I thought in my head.

"I'm just scared to do it wrong again. I can't keep wasting my time. I want this to be right because it feels right, but I also don't want to get my heart broke again." I admitted.

"He's afraid of the same thing. At any moment you feel like it's hurting you more than doing you good walk away. Until then, don't make it hard on y'all. Enjoy it because if it's meant for you, it'll be for you. And the last thing you want to do is lose a man over you being scared of his love then you'll watch him love someone else like he was trying to love you." She schooled me.

I sat in one of the chairs and thought about what she and

Amelia said. Dre made my heart melt when he stepped in the room. He made me want more and to do better so I could be perfect for him. And even the days where I wasn't perfect or dressed, he made me feel like the most amazing woman in the world, and my kids liked him so far. I wasn't messing that up, and as long as he didn't, either we would be good. Hopefully one day he wanted what I did, and we could have that happily ever after love.

22

DRE

I was back at work and wishing that I could go back to the few days that had just passed. Aleah and I were able to take the kids out to the new nickelodeon park before we had to drop them back off home and they had a blast. I just knew Shay would have called me with some bullshit because Dream told her everything, but she didn't. In fact, she was a little happy that I had someone Dream spoke about so much. I had given her some extra money, and she was happy with that.

My office door opened, and the new girl that would be working as my assistant walked in. She came in with a coffee and a smile. As a man, I had to look at her, and I smiled at what I saw. Her tall frame was probably due to the heels she had on, and her pantsuit fit her body perfectly. I could tell by her thighs that she had ass behind her. She wasn't the prettiest in the face, but she also wasn't the ugliest. She had a small gap in between her two front teeth and a beauty mark next to her top lip.

"Good morning, here's your coffee. I hope I made it right?" She smiled.

"Thanks, umm? What was your name again?"

"Michelle, and you're welcome, you need me to do anything else for you, love?" She questioned.

"No, thank you," I said, looking up from my computer screen at Aleah who was walking through the door.

"Okay, call if you need me to do anything," Michelle said and walked away.

Aleah closed the door behind her and turned and looked at me with a frown. My baby was jealous and for no reason.

"You better tell her to cut the pet names short. With her giant ass, don't play with me. The only reason I ain't say nothing cause this your job. I brought your smiling ass some lunch." She frowned, tossing the bag on my desk.

"Ain't your ass supposed to be at work?" I asked her.

"I have the late shifts this week. I'm doing three to eleven. Which is why I'm in my work clothes, I figured I'd bring your ass lunch before I went in since you said you would be staying in late today." She said sitting in my lap.

"Thank you bestie, you need some money so you can order lunch or you made you some too?" I asked her.

"No I don't need your money, and that coffee to dark you like yours brown like me. Don't drink that shit." She said, throwing the cup in the trash.

"I don't even drink coffee in the afternoon so you know I wasn't going to drink it. I asked her if she could bring something for me to drink from the store when she went and I guess she thought I wanted that." I said.

"And why does your ass need an assistant anyway? You've been doing your job good alone from what you told me." She asked.

"Cause Mr. Harold was saying something bout a promotion. In the new position, I would need one, so he hired her and told me to get her ready now. once I switch over, that's one less thing I have to worry about. And neither do you, I know we are rocking with this bestie thing but ain't no other bitch got my attention and I ain't trying to give it to them. I like how my bestie treats me. What would be good is if you stop holding out on that pussy. You gone give me some then take it back like that, it ain't cool. Every time I touch you, I am ready to slide up in you." I professed.

"Oh god, have ever was told you got that kind of dick that makes a bitch go crazy? If not, then you do. That's why I gotta make sure I keep my distance from you. Plus I don't want to ruin things, they're too perfect. You know you mean a lot to me, and before we get crazy, I want to make sure everything on my end is out of the way." She spoke about her divorce.

Letting out a chuckle I didn't even bother to continue the conversation. With her sitting on my lap, I pulled out my highlighter and continued to highlight the numbers that went up. She must have caught on because she stood up and grabbed her bag.

"See this is what I didn't want to do," she said to me.

I continued my work because the conversation was pointless, and I didn't know how she acted when she was mad, and Shay had already brought enough drama here.

"So you gone ignore me." She asked, grabbing my face and lifting my head to look at her.

"I ain't ignoring you, but what the fuck you want me to say, I understand cause I don't. One minute you all over me and the next you wanna friend zone me. Like at this point let's make the shit clear cause I ain't bout to keep telling you I want you for you to bring up that fucking divorce like you guilty of the shit we doing cause of that. Fuck that divorce I don't give a fuck about it as long as when the time comes you make the moves to get that shit out the way and Id rather it be sooner than later, but I want you to do it and make sure that's what you want to do. You the one that ain't take steps to do it and you know he won't. What we not bout to do is keep playing with each other's feelings. I know I mean a lot to you, and you mean that much more to me. I honestly grew to love your stupid ass, and you keep going with this friend shit. I like that I'm your best friend that means we did shit the right way by being friends first and learning everything there is to know bout each other. Our foundation is solid now it's time to build on that shit." I let out.

"Damn," Aleah said, wiping the tears that fell from her eyes.

Shaking my head, I kissed her goodbye and got back to work. I was going over our client's files and seeing their progress for the last month. I also had new potential investors, and with that, I knew I would be in the office until around six or later so I was glad that she had brought me food at first, but now I was wishing she didn't. She hadn't even acknowledged the fact that I said I loved her. And I wished that I hadn't said anything. She had me out here feeling like a sucka.

Slamming the highlighter down I sat back in my chair. It was time for me to get my shit in check and stop acting like I was hurting for love. If she wanted me like I thought she did, she would come around, and if not I would show her that I could really be just friends with her.

23

LEAH

"I had to have dropped you." My mom told me as she paced the floor in my living room.

I was telling her all about Dre and I's week and how he barely talked to me in the last three days. I was laid on my couch with my feet up tired from work, and she wanted to talk.

"I do not understand why you are doing this, that man is for you. hell I can tell. You only stay home on the weekends because you're laid up at his house like you live there. You make sure you take this man lunch every day before you go to work and if you have the morning shift, you make sure it's in the fridge the night before. You wash his clothes, clean his house. And even bust it open for him at his mommas. You've met the lady, she calls you her future daughter in law, as well as met his child and introduced him to yours. Spent the night with your kids at his mother's house. He's offered to pay for your house when you didn't have it, he offers you money everyday. And his dick good, and you keep him in the friend zone because of a nigga who ain't shit and what he's done to you? They ain't the same person, so he doesn't deserve to get treated as such. Yes, you are scared, but if you don't take the risk, you'll never know." She sighed, taking the seat next to me.

"I just don't want to lose him altogether if this happens and it doesn't work out. I not only lose him, but I lose my best friend. I can't take that, I love that he's been there and he's talked me through a lot. He listens to me and doesn't judge me. I can't risk that for a relationship that may not work out." I cried.

"He sounds perfect."

"That's the point most men who seem perfect got a lot of shit that comes behind them and they usually the worst ones. Then you and Amelia making it like it's my fault and his ass won't even talk to me. I've been home for the last few days, and I want to be with him. My home on weekdays is usually with him. I almost was late for work this week twice because I'm used to his black ass waking me up for work, now I have to do it on my own." I went on.

"Then go there make him talk to you, he's probably tired of expressing his feelings only to get them dumb ass responses from you. Tell that man how you really feel about him and don't hold out cause he ain't did that shit to you. Girl, why God ain't send me no damn man like that. I'd probably be kissing the fucking ground he walked on, hell and even if he did fuck up long as he don't get to carried away I would forgive his fine ass and wish somebody would say something. Hell if my man says he sorry bitch he sorry. I forgive him and forget what I told you cause I might need to tell you again and don't want you looking at me like I'm stupid." She said, making me laugh.

"You right, I'm gone get my man. His ass at work and I know he in a meeting he told me last weekend he had a meeting today. I drove by his house a few nights after I got off and his car don't be out front like it usually does so I'm gone reach out to him, and hopefully, I can swing by after work and make things up to him." I told my mom.

Since everyone was always at her house, and the process of it being renovated started, she damn near lived at my house. So while I was gone for the week, she would be at my place then go home on the weekends.

My mom turned the tv on, and I closed my eyes to take a nap until it was time for me to go to work. I hated working the late shifts, but I didn't complain about work because I loved the money. Instead of falling asleep I laid there thinking about Dre's chocolate ass. If I told it right I loved him too, yet when he said it, he said it with a bunch of things I didn't want to hear about myself, so it was hard for me to respond. I also didn't want him to see my cry over him, so the best thing for me to do was leave. Had I known me leaving out his office without a better response to him would have led us here, I would have poured my heart out to him.

I tried multiple times to fall asleep, but I couldn't Dre kept popping up in my mind and something was telling me if I didn't fix things I would lose a great man and I wasn't willing to give that up. Opening up my phone, I wrote him a bunch of text messages explaining how I felt. Yet instead of sending them, I erased them and kept trying over and over to find the perfect words to say.

Going to my closet, I got out my laptop and began to look for divorce lawyers. I even called a few and got prices while looking at their reviews. If anything was going to show him I was serious I knew this would. After talking to a few, I got my things and headed out for work. Before I put my phone up I sent him a text, I wanted him to talk to me.

Bestie- I love you too.

I saw that he read the message; however, he didn't respond. A few times the bubbles popped up like he was going to, but then they went away.

From Bestie- You better, now bring your ass home after work.

I smiled at his response and put my phone up. I was definitely taking my ass home to him where I belonged.

24

DRE

I walked over to Leah and her sister's table. Pulling her up and kissing her on the lips right there in front of her sister. I thought she would pull away; instead, she held on to my face and slipped her tongue into my mouth, making my dick grow.

"You trying to give me blue balls?" I asked boldly.

"Shut up." She smiled, placing her face into my chest.

"Well damn sis, that's what the fuck I'm talking bout." Amelia piped her up.

Stepping back from Leah, I allowed her to sit back down. I slid in the booth next to her and wrapped my arm around her shoulder.

"What's up Mi?" I grinned at her sister like I knew her my whole life.

When really this was my second or third time seeing her ass in person.

"What's up, bro? I was just telling this bitch y'all do too much to be best friends, but y'all keep running with it." She replied.

"She knows what's up, and she loves me either way. I only came over here because she was playing with me on some I ain't gone see her until next week shit. I ain't with that. I know when she gets the kids, she stays away from me. I respect that, but she ain't got them yet. My cousin told me to tell you wassup too." I said all in one breath.

"I done told that little ass boy he ain't got enough money for me, and even if he did, he would need to go to the dentist first and get that mouth figured out. Plus I'm a hoe, I'll ruin his life. Y'all good people and I'd rather keep it that way. I don't trick in the family. He'd be around too much and know too much. But put your foot down, don't let her play with you like that." She laughed.

Amelia was cool as hell, and she wasn't afraid to let it be known who she was. I, for one, didn't think she was a hoe, but of course, I didn't know her well enough to know the truth. Let her tell it she was, and Leah would just laugh like it was funny.

"I got to get back to work, take care of my baby for me, Amelia. And Leah tell that man you taken 'cause if I see another kissy face on your screen Ima break that bitch." I said, standing up.

She looked down at her phone and cleared the screen. Her ass must have forgotten she was texting. However, I was dead serious about breaking it if she continued on with that shit. I would just get her another one and change the number.

"You ain't breaking shit." She kissed her teeth.

Bending down, I grabbed her by her chin, forcing her to look me in the eyes. She tried to pull away, but that only made me squeeze a little tighter. She bit down on her bottom lip and closed her eyes with her sexy ass.

"You want to try me and see how that shit turn out? Don't fucking play with me or my emotions cause I ain't playing with yours. Now dead that shit or you gone cause a lot of problems not only for you but that nigga too you feel me." I shot before kissing her lips and walking away.

"Got damn, bitch. I know that shit got yo pussy wet cause you like that crazy shit. Make me want to get me a man that's gone threaten me while looking at me with so much love." Amelia yelled out, causing me to laugh.

Turning to look back, I noticed a guy walked over to their table and say something to Leah that caused her to frown. I quickly made my way back around and caught a bit of their conversation.

"That's who you got my kids around?" I heard.

Leah opened her mouth and then closed it once she saw the frown attached to my face.

"Aye, back up for me." I tapped him, causing him to turn towards me.

"Fuck you mean back up? That's my wife nigga." He told me.

"Yeah, that's all cool, but not for much longer. Now, like I said back up out of her personal space for me. I don't know what you on but clearly, she ain't on that. Now man to man, if you feeling aggressive you can take that up with me but she a whole female." I replied calmly.

"Quanny, it's cool. I got this go back to work." Aleah pleaded.

"Nah, let Nymir talk to him since he wanted to know about him," Amelia called out.

"So what you want to do? Cause I'm not no bitch feel me?" Nymir challenged.

"I don't feel you, and we can do whatever you want to do. If you got any questions though I'm here, so ask me don't ask her. Now we can talk like men, or we can act crazy either way is cool with me. I'm on a time limit though so think quick before I walk away, and they are coming with me." I stepped closer to him.

"Leah, fuck you yo. You can get that divorce too." He called before turning to walk off.

I waited for him to walk towards the exit I made sure they were okay before I headed back into work to sit in my last meeting. Mr. Harold talked our heads off while I texted Leah, making sure she knew that I wasn't playing with her.

"DreQuan I hope you pay attention." Mr. Harold called out, causing everyone to look at me.

"I heard you loud and clear, sir," I stated even though I felt like this meeting was something I shouldn't have had to attend.

I was never late to work, and I pulled more hours than most people. I also met with clients daily, and most of them were great investments. However, I still showed respect and came to the meeting like everyone else.

"I also would like to get a cleaning done. We have been experiencing some little mice running around, with that said, please try and keep your offices as clean as possible. I will now be having my assistant do walk-throughs at least twice a week to ensure you aren't leaving any trash or food in your office and keeping things clean around your space. Everyone have a blessed and safe day, and well you know the saying you ain't gotta go but get the heck up out of here." He finished up.

I stood up and left out, I was done for the day, and I was coming out of the suit so I could turn up. Dream and my mom had spent the weekend at Disney World and wouldn't return back until the morning, and I planned on having a little fun until it was time to pick them up.

I hopped in my car not being one to text and drive, so I tossed my phone into the cup holder. Pulling off and swinging through the hood was something that was becoming foreign to me. So I took that route instead of heading straight home.

Every block was full of people out playing cards or cooking out while the kids ran freely. That was one of the many things I enjoyed about being in the projects. Even when you thought it was nothing to do, you could always come outside and either play or watch some shit go down. It wasn't always safe, but it was home and if you were from there wasn't anybody from any other hood coming and you was fighting by yourself. Tasker was like a dysfunctional family, everybody slept with everybody so somehow someway most of the kids were family, and even if the moms hated each other the kids still played, and the men showed love.

I parked and let my window down. Don's boy Juice walked up to my car and stuck his head inside.

"Damn old head, I've been trying to see you since the ball game. It's been a while, My G, on the real I just wanted to thank you. That day you tossed me that couple hundred I was in a jam. I took a major loss, my bitch got hit with an eviction notice so of course, I handled that, but then my baby needed diapers and milk. That shit took a chunk out of my pockets. My Re-Up money was gone, and I knew I would have to either pull overtime at my job or on the block only for my job to get closed down by LNI that night. Making the decision for me, I got a new job though delivering for a pizza store, and the block was jumping but product ain't the same, slowing the money down. I ain't trying to step out and get me a new plug, but it's looking drastic for me. I got about six something to my name, but I want to pay you back man." He said, reaching into his pocket.

"Don't worry about that, you keep that and use it to do what you got to do, just keep me in mind when you make it up out of this bitch."

Most times, I wanted my money back and tripled, in this case, it felt good just to know I had blessed someone in a time of need. God was gone look out for me, and that was the only pack back a nigga like me needed.

"I got you bro, On my mama when I get right, you gone be the first person I holla at," Juice promised.

"Bet, take care of yourself," I told him.

He nodded and walked off, climbing out of the car I made my rounds. It seemed like I was gone forever how everybody was acting once they saw me.

"Damn, Dre. Them suits got you looking good as hell. I mean not that you weren't already fine as hell." One of the young girls flirted.

"Excuse me, I'm just trying to get in the store." Stepping around her, I went to get the things I came in for.

"Oh you too good for us now, cause back in the day my mom

was getting you right." She snapped, rolling her eyes and neck.

"That's the thing if your moms was getting me right, fuck I look like entertaining your young ass." I snapped back.

That was one of the things that could never be understood. These girls was fine with fucking someone that had run through their family just so they can feel up at the moment. When the whole time they just be another bitch added to the list if they even remembered.

"Opp." She said while grabbing her chest like she was hurt.

I got my things paid for and headed out of the store. There was no point in continuing any conversation with her, and she ruined my mood. So instead of swinging by the other blocks, my ass headed home.

"Couple niggas might done had it but it still grip tight. If you gettin' to a bag, you the hot girl type

Four hundred degrees, I ain't Juvenile. D'usse got her goin' wild" my head bobbed to the lyrics of *all dat* song.

I had to laugh because if Leah was around, she would have rapped Meghan's part while my part would have been money bag. Though we had sex once, the tension was high, and ever since we been to the club that one time this song became a part of our friendship. Everybody had songs, and we didn't have a slow song just yet all we had was this.

Pulling up to my house, I hopped out and went inside to get dressed. Leah had picked out my outfit for me the night before since she not only was my personal chef; she was my stylist too. That girl eased her way in my life and fucked up cause it was no way she was leaving. We would be friends until the day I died if she didn't end up being my wife. She was someone I could honestly say I saw a future with and I was glad we became friends first and got to know each other.

Going into the bathroom, I turned the shower water on to let it heat up. The music cut on from the speakers and pandora played Brian McKnight. This had to be some shit that girl left on because I would have never. Stepping into the shower, I quickly washed my body. Just like any other time, Leah entered my mind, and I instantly bricked up.

Her curvy body and soft lips did something to me, I grabbed my soldier and stroked him until I was releasing in the shower water.

"Got damn. I need some pussy." I groaned once I caught my breath.

I had to shower once more before getting out, drying off and brushing my teeth. Making my way into my room with my towel wrapped around my waist, I found myself humming to a Monica song. Stepping into a pair of Ethika boxers followed by a white pair of True Religion jeans and a white button-down Armani shirt. I fixed my collar and then slid my Rolex watch on my wrist. I took pride in that watch because that was the first thing flashy I bought myself once I started seeing some real legal money. Deciding on wearing my white Alexander McQueen sneakers, I stepped my feet into them.

"Yeah a nigga was fly as fuck" I thought while brushing my waves.

I checked my phone and to see that it was a little after nine and Don was on his way to the club where we was supposed to meet. Not wanting to be the late one I grabbed my wallet and headed out the door.

🍂

"THIS JAWN PACKED AS HELL, AND MOST OF THE BITCHES ARE hit. I wouldn't fuck them with three condoms. Well some of them ain't that bad." Don laughed.

He was drunk as hell and trying to find something to take home. Meanwhile, I on the other hand, only had about two drinks. Drinking and driving wasn't one of the things I liked to partake in.

"Bro, grab that one right there," Juice said while pulling a girl to the side.

His ass knew he had a family at home. I wasn't going to stop him because that was his choice if he wanted to risk it all. On another day I would talk to him about it and see where his head was really at. I knew for a fact with the occupation he had the last thing he wanted was a hurt girl willing to hurt him back.

A few strippers came over and began to dance. I had grabbed a thousand ones at the door, so I was throwing them all over the place. Strippers made me happy, and so the turn up was becoming real.

Awhile went by, and I decided it was time to go. When we left the club the sun was coming up, and I was dead tired. We said our goodbyes and I got into my car and pulled off.

I was fighting to keep my eyes open, so I let the windows down to get some air. The UPS truck in front of me kept switching lanes and picking up speed. I sped up to go around it, but just as I got close enough to pass it, the truck went to switch lanes again. I pressed lightly on the brakes I watched as the truck got close to a car and went to change lanes; again. However, a car was coming up, and it must have not seen it. The truck moved over and hit the car, causing the car behind it to slam into it. I pressed my brakes but wasn't fast enough. The truck spent a little, and the back swung slamming into the front of my car. I heard a kid cry and looked over. My vision was blurry, but I could have sworn that I was looking at Aleah's son. I tried to get out of the car, but I felt too weak. My head was spinning, and while reaching for the door, I noticed my chair was pushed into my back seat.

The more I tried to get out the more dizzy I became. I wiped whatever was dripping into my eyes and kept pushing at the door. I noticed my hands were covered in blood. Indicating that my head was bleeding. In that moment, panic took over. I kicked at the window, and as soon as it broke, I tried to climb out. It took me some time, but I was able to get out of the car. I went to get to the kids, and as soon as I took one step, everything went black.

✵ 25 ✵

LEAH

"Aleah, we need you to stay. We have an overload of patients in the waiting room, and it's not enough staff to cover for the front. You'll get paid time and a half for the over-time." My boss Susie said to me just as I went to clock out.

"Susie, you know my situation with the kids I'm supposed to get them tonight. I'll have to call and see if someone can get them just until I get off." I told her with a long sigh.

"Thank you so much. I'll give you an extra day off next weekend when you have to get them, now please hurry with the phone call and get back up front, I also may need you on regis-tration for a while." She gave me a weak smile.

I nodded my head and pulled my cell out to call my Amelia.

"Sis, I have to do a double, so I need you to go to my house and grab the kids. You can either take them to your house or stay there with them just until I get off." I begged.

"I got you, don't work too hard boo." She replied.

"Love you," I replied before hanging up.

I sent Nymir a text telling him that Amelia would be waiting for him before I went back to the front desk. For some reason, when it got hot, we would always have more patients than normal all over the hospital.

"I guess they pulled you for another shift too?" Julie said when I sat back down.

"Girl yes and I swear I don't want to be here. I do need this time and a half though." I said while grabbing a stack of papers to help with registrations.

"It's been a whole bunch of shooting victims as well as other shit like always. Kynisha did a no call no show and Jessie's daughter is in the hospital with the flu." Julie let me know.

"That's messed up," I replied before checking someone in.

For most of my shift, I spent my time between checking people in and doing registration. Soon as I felt like we were done a shit load of patients came in. People were coming in for anything like colds, headaches, anything.

"I need a fucking break at this point hell even the nurses ain't going home." I yawned.

I was fighting my sleep, so I went to the break room and got a cup of coffee. I sent Quanny a text telling him I was doing a double and do not wait up for my phone call. He quickly replied and told me to call him when I got off.

I knew he had gone out with his cousins, and I wish I could have gone with him. Since I had started to get the kids for three days out of the week, I hadn't been out. Amelia was complaining now because if my days were spent with the kids, I was somewhere with my Quanny just talking and having fun. I was falling for him way faster then I would like because I was afraid he could hurt me just like the last person. The many kisses we shared did something to my soul, and it was almost as if he was supposed to be mine. One of the things that was stopping us was the fact that Nymir was pushing off the divorce. He figured we could make things work and it didn't help that I didn't have a good lawyer—one who knew what he was doing.

"I know you need a break, but Julie is doing registrations, and it's nobody up at the front doing check-ins." The security guard informed me.

"Okay." I followed behind him with my coffee and sat down to do the rest of the check-ins.

Julie came back, and we took turns one of us would go register patients, while the other would check-in. Seven in the morning finally came around, and I was damn near running so that I could get my things and go.

I looked at my phone and saw that Amelia texted me around three in the morning saying Nymir never came with the kids. I scrolled to my messages from him only for him to tell me he never had any plans on bringing them and that they would be headed home from Wildwood this morning. So it was fine that I was doing a double. I called him to confirm if I could still get them today. Since we had been going through court, he had been following the directions of the judge, and we had been co-parenting really well. I was hoping he wasn't back on his bullshit because as far as the kids we were good, and I was happy with that.

I grabbed my bags and walked back out to the front. Continuously checking my phone for a response.

"Have a good day, Leah. See you on Monday." The security guard told me, waving bye.

"See you Monday," I replied, just as the ambulance pulled in.

They hopped out and pulled a stretcher from the back by the way they were moving I just knew somebody was extremely hurt. I watched slowly as the face of the person came out and I had to do a double-take.

"Twenty-eight-year-old male, in a car crash on the highway. He's suffering head trauma his car flipped and is totaled. His name on his ID says DreQuan-" before they could finish a scream left my mouth that I didn't know I was capable of letting out.

"Oh, God, is he okay. That's my boyfriend." I screamed to the paramedic as he rushed Dre inside.

They ignored me as they held the oxygen mask on his face

and rushed him through the side doors. I ran back inside the hospital and went to the front desk.

"Precious, I need you to look up this information for me. Give me the emergency contact number that's listed, please. It should say, Carmen." I told my friend who I had become close with.

My hands were shaking, and I'm sure I was ugly from crying. I gave her everything I knew about DreQuan, his first and last name and birthday. I knew it wasn't much but being as though I was sure someone was in the back putting in his information it would pop up. After a few seconds she ran off his emergency contact number, and I was able to call Ms Carmen. Walking outside to get a breath of fresh air, I waited for her to answer.

"Hello, good morning. Who is this." She said, sounding like I had woken her up.

"Hey, Ms Carmen, it's Leah. Quanny, I mean DreQuan's friend. I'm at work down here at University hospital, and they just rushed him in. I'm not sure his condition, but they did say he was in a car crash." I told her.

She got to yelling and screaming about her baby. Everything else went unheard as I watched two ambulances flying down the street. One stopped at children's which was right next door and swung the back doors open. While the other stopped a few feet from me.

"Hello, hello, are you there." I heard as I watched them pull Nymir from one ambulance and Callie from the other.

"I'm cool man, let me go over and see my kids." Nymir tried to get up.

Everything was moving in slow motion as I watched them rush her inside. Another scream left my mouth, and finally my feet began to move. I ran over while they ran her inside following close behind them.

"Please tell me what happened to my baby. Please, what's going on where is my son? Help me somebody help me." I yelled out.

"Ma'am you have to let them do their job." A lady pulled me back saying something I was all too familiar with saying to other people.

"I need to know what is going on, that's my baby. Where is my son, please find my son. God please, I can't do this, I can't take this." I fell on to the floor and cried.

There was nothing I could do, and nobody seemed to be helping me. I stayed on the floor, begging God to help me.

"Why would you do this to me, God don't take them from me," I begged while bawling.

Snot was coming from my nose, and I couldn't find it in me to call anyone. Just when I felt like things couldn't get any worse, I watched as another ambulance pulled up. In my gut, I knew to get up and check for Cion.

I walked to the emergency entrance and watched as they opened up the back doors. This time the doctors came running out. My stomach began to hurt, and my breath felt like it was caught in my throat. The doctors jumped in the back of the ambulance and yelled out Code Blue. They pulled the gurney out, and I watched them do CPR on my baby. My knees got weak, and I fell to the ground, hitting my head on something. I laid there asking God to work on my kids as my heart felt like it would pound out of my chest. I failed my kids. I wasn't there to protect them, and Dre, on the other hand, I couldn't even be there for him. This was all too much. I began to hyperventilate, and I closed my eyes and welcomed the darkness.

To Be Continued

Cole Hart
SIGNATURE NOVELS

THANK YOU

To our loyal Cole Hart Signature readers,

Cole Hart Signature is always growing and changing. Some of you have been following Cole Hart since the beginning of his career, while others have seen us go from Cole Hart Presents to Cole Hart Signature. Then there are our daily new supporters who've only known us for what we are as a company today. Despite our changes, how or when you became a fanatic, we want to kindly thank you for the support.

We appreciate all our Cole Hart Readers because without every single one of you, we wouldn't be the company we are today.

If this book is your first introduction to our company, welcome! And be sure to sign up for email list by click the link, http://bit.ly/2BtGCXH, and joining out text-mail list by texting Cole-HartSig to (855)231-5230. Cole Hart Signature also has a Facebook group where fans get to discuss the plot, characters, overall releases about their favorite book. If itching for new and interesting conversation, click the link, https://geni.us/ColeHartSignatureRead, to join today!

Lastly, Cole Hart Signature is always interested in partnering with aspiring authors, new or experienced, who thrive in the African Urban Fiction and Romance Fiction genre. If you're interested in joining our team, go to www.colehartsignature.com/submissions.

Once again, we truly appreciate all the support over the years.

Much Love,
    CHS

AN AMERICAN HUSTLER

Click the link to stay up to date: https://www.colehartsignature.com/an-american-hustler/